ENJOY ALL OF THE BOOKS IN
THE GUARDIANS *of* GA'HOOLE SERIES!

Broken Talon Point

Northern Kingdoms

ninsula
the
rit Woods

Ice
Narrows

Sea of Hoolemere

ape
aux

Island of Hoole

The Beaks

sert
of
eer

Forest Kingdom
of Tyto

River Hoole

Soren's Hollow

"Madame, may I be of service? You seem most distressed."

*It was a gentleman speaking, no doubt about that,
Madame Plonk thought.*

GUARDIANS
of GA'HOOLE

BOOK TWELVE

The Golden Tree

BY KATHRYN LASKY

SCHOLASTIC INC.

New York Toronto London Auckland Sydney
Mexico City New Delhi Hong Kong Buenos Aires

ISBN-13: 978-0-439-88806-6
ISBN-10: 0-439-88806-9

Text copyright © 2007 by Kathryn Lasky

Artwork by Richard Cowdrey
Design by Steve Scott

12 11 10 9 8 7 6 5 4 3 2   7 8 9 10 11 12/0

Printed in the U.S.A.   40

First printing, March 2007

Contents

Prologue

"*Look at me, look at me!*" *the Great Gray hooted. His primaries sparkled silver in the moonlight as he carved a steep turn, then folded his wings and plunged toward a cresting wave. He swooped up, barely escaping the grip of the sea as the spume trailed behind him like a comet's tail. Twilight looked to the rest of the Band.* "*And they say seagulls do it better!*"

Gylfie turned to Soren, and Digger sighed then churred softly. "*We all know what's coming, don't we?*

"*Indeed!*" *Soren and Digger both said at once. Then Twilight began:*

I don't just do it better
I don't even get wetter
I'm prettier — hey, beautiful!
I'm a gorgeous owl and not a gull!
Waves crash, grass grows
I can whup anything before it knows.

The winds were capricious at this time of year and the owls of the Band entertained themselves by sliding in and out of their folds, rising and plummeting on the rogue drafts that buffeted the Island of Hoole.

There was nothing that owls liked doing more than playing with air, with wind, and none did it better than the Band. Despite the season, almost winter and the beginning of what the owls of the Great Ga'Hoole Tree called the time of the white rain, the great tree still retained the nearly golden glow of summer. It had remained this way ever since Coryn, the new young king, had retrieved the Ember of Hoole several moon cycles ago from the volcano in Beyond the Beyond.

Soren glanced toward the tree nervously. Its strange defiance of the seasons did not disturb him as much as knowing that his dear nephew, Coryn, was in his hollow, brooding. It was understandable that the responsibilities of kingship weighed heavily on the young owl, but Soren knew that it was the ember itself that added immeasurably to Coryn's anxieties.

Inside his rather modest hollow in the tree, the young king peered into the glow of the ember, the Ember of Hoole. Orange with a lick of blue at its center ringed with green, it was no simple coal, and he did not see simple things in it. Coryn was a flame reader, but reading the flames of a fire was different from understanding the shifting intensities of this ember. The images it yielded, like those of the flames, came without being beckoned, but they were more powerful than flame visions, often warped and not to be completely trusted. What the young Barn Owl was seeing now made his heart race and his gizzard quake. Peering into its flickering blue center he glimpsed a spot of white that grew rounder and larger. Like a moon, he thought. Like . . . a seam slants across the white sphere. . . . Like . . . like a scar. . . . Like my scar. No, not mine. NYRA's!

CHAPTER ONE

A Golden Glow

"Coryn, you look as if you've just seen a scroom." It was midday and most owls at the great tree were fast asleep. Soren, Coryn's uncle and chief counselor, had just entered the hollow.

"If only she was just that — a scroom." Coryn looked up from the ember in its teardrop-shaped iron cask that Bubo the blacksmith had made.

So it's Nyra again! Soren thought. There had been no sign of Nyra or any of the Pure Ones since Coryn had retrieved the ember and defeated the Pure Ones in the Beyond. Nyra had escaped. Most owls believed that she was as good as dead, her troops virtually destroyed, and the ember safe in the talons of Coryn, a youthful but canny leader. The balance of power had at last changed. But Coryn was still haunted by her, and he imagined always would be, whether she was dead or alive. Of late he had become even more obsessed. Soren studied his dear nephew as the young owl peered into the glow of the

1

ember. His heart went out to him and he felt a sorrowful twinge in his gizzard. The scar that slashed Coryn's face — a wound inflicted by his own mother — seemed to twitch in a private agony. He felt compelled to address Coryn directly now about this obsession. Perhaps getting it out in the open would be a good thing.

"Coryn, first of all, there is no evidence that she still is alive. And second, even if she is, with her forces all but annihilated she can be of little danger."

Coryn jerked his head around, unlocking his gaze from the glow. "But Uncle, Nyra is no mere evil owl, and if . . ."

"And if," Soren broke in testily. "I know, Coryn. I read the legends, too. If she is a hagsfiend . . ."

"No, Uncle. Perhaps not a full-blown hagsfiend but a relic from that ancient time who, through some twist of fate or nachtmagen, was reborn into this one. And if this is true . . ." He hesitated. "Well, you know what I said when we finished reading the first legend of Grank the Collier."

Yes, Soren knew. Coryn had concluded that if his mother had the taint of a hagsfiend's blood then his own blood must be cursed as well. It was idiotic, but no matter how often Soren reassured him, Coryn could not be convinced. Luckily, none of the rest of the Band nor Otulissa knew of Coryn's fears. The last thing Coryn wanted revealed was that he might be the offspring of a hags-fiend.

"So you saw something in the glow of the ember, I assume?" Soren asked.

Coryn looked up and blinked with a sudden curiosity. "Why are you here with me and not in your own hollow with Pelli and your little chicks? It's daytime. You should be sleeping."

"I'm not sure."

"A dream?" Coryn asked.

"Maybe." Soren shut his eyes for several seconds as if seeking patience or perhaps the right words. "You know how it is. . . . You have firesight and I have starsight."

"But starsight is when you dream about things that sometimes then happen. I don't understand what you are saying. You dreamed about me finding images in the ember? The images of my mother? Then you might well know why I am disturbed."

"Yes. I dreamed. But I don't quite understand the dreams myself." Soren sighed. He had been asleep in the cozy hollow that he shared with his mate, Pelli, and their three little chicks, Sebastiana, or "Basha" for short, Blythe, and Bell, when suddenly he realized that he was not in his own dream but another's — or perhaps sharing

Coryn's waking visions as he glimpsed them in the ember. It had rather unnerved Soren, because in the legends they had read that Kreeth, the infamous hagsfiend of ancient times, had an ability to do just this: to enter other creatures' dreams. Soren, however, was certain that it was starsight that he had experienced. Starsight was a peculiar and very rare phenomenon in which the stars in some mysterious way illuminated an owl's dream. Most creatures thought that during the day, when nocturnal animals slept, stars vanished, but for some they did not. The stars became little holes in the fabric of their dreams and through these holes they saw things that often came true.

And he had seen Coryn's vision, though it was not a dream of a terrible moon that turned into a scarred face, or of flames and fear and terrible loss. It was like fragments of a vision within a vision, a dream within a dream. But did this mean that Nyra still lived? Would she come to kill her only son? Soren did not want to betray the slightest hint of fear or worry. This was a magnificent time for the great tree and for the young king. "As I said," Soren began to speak with renewed firmness in his voice, "you have no evidence that she's still alive. Nor do you have any that she is a hagsfiend. She's just a miserable, evil owl. No more. No less."

"Maybe a little bit more," Coryn said softly.

"What do you mean?"

"Soren, when we were reading those legends, especially the parts about the hagsfiends — particularly Kreeth, when she was angered by Lutta — it reminded me . . ."

"Reminded you of what?" Soren asked quietly. The glow of the ember cast deep red shadows that leaped through the air of the hollow in a wild and antic dance.

"It reminded me of my mother. When I was very young and she would get angry with me her face seemed to grow even bigger. There was a darkness like shadows beneath the white feathers of her face and her wings darkened near the edges, too, and seemed to hang like rags, torn and crowish. You know how crows' wings are ragged? At the time I thought it was my imagination, but while we were reading the legends and the descriptions of hagsfiends I kept thinking, 'This is familiar, I know this from somewhere.' The blood, the violence I learned of in those legends reminded me of a time in my own life: the Tupsi that required me to kill someone dear and close to me. And with my mother, as with Kreeth, it was not so much hate but the absence of any truly owlish feeling. She was so haggish."

Soren remained silent for a while. Perhaps the young king was right, but it would do him no good to brood endlessly about his origins and his inheritance. *Blood hardly defines one's character. We are made by our actions, not our blood,* Soren thought. And Coryn was an owl of extraordinary courage, insight, wisdom and, most important, compassion. He of all owls had triumphed over the meanness of his life, the brutality of his upbringing. If he had haggish blood in his veins, he still had the noblest of gizzards.

Outside a bitter wind blew and, although it was midday, it might as well have been night for the sky roiled with dark storm clouds. It was odd that even though it was now the season of the white rain, the milkberries that normally turned white had a new luminous glow more reminiscent of summer and the time of the golden rain. Perhaps most curious of all, however, was that although many of the leaves of the great tree had fallen as always at this time of year, they had left behind a shimmering shadow of themselves. And some had not fallen at all, and still retained a golden splendor. The owls of the tree marveled at this peculiar phenomenon, exclaiming that it was like an endless summer. But Soren found this gilded beauty mildly disturbing. The shimmering nimbus of light that shone from where a leaf had fallen reminded him of scrooms, the unsettled spirits of dead owls that lurked until all their unfinished business on Earth was concluded.

The young king and his uncle Soren were silent, enveloped in the soft glow that streamed from the ember's teardrop-shaped cask. For several minutes, the two owls stood with their faces tipped toward the light of the ember, each alone in his thoughts. Most likely those thoughts were similar. Although they had read about the power of the ember in the legends, they knew it was not merely legendary. Its magic, with all of its good and its bad possibilities, was very real. With the ember came great blessings as well as grave dangers. When the ember had been retrieved after a thousand years, they both suspected that a small gash had been torn in the very fabric of the owl universe, an opening through which nachtmagen could seep.

Nyra was the very embodiment of evil, but there had always been evil. Coryn wondered if, with this small rip in the world of the owls, Nyra could gain a talon-hold through nachtmagen. And if she *did* have even a taint of hagsfiend blood, would this nachtmagen give her the powers of a creature such as Kreeth, the arch hagsfiend of the ancient world? In the legends, Kreeth — with her weird incantations and experiments — had created some truly horrendous monstrosities. Could Nyra perhaps be a descendant of one of her last and more successful experiments? Worse, even, than a simple hagsfiend?

That was precisely what worried Coryn. For what did that make him? This secret fear festered in him, haunted him, and caused him endless agony.

Soren's reading of the legends, however, had given him other concerns and other truths. In his gizzard, he knew that the most important lesson of the legends was to embrace reason and not magic, good or bad. He understood Coryn's obsession with his heritage, but he also knew that Coryn was intrinsically good. To rely on magic, or to become obsessed with the ember could only distract Coryn from the responsibilities of his role as king. To be a true Guardian of the great tree had always been considered every bit as noble as being its king. But it was up to the king to instill this sense of nobility — and to lead. In the oath of the Guardians of the Great Ga'Hoole Tree, there was nothing about magic. And the notion of nobility through royal birth was rejected. The words of the oath that Soren had taken so many years before coursed through his mind and set his gizzard aquiver: *I am the eyes in the night, the silence within the wind. I am the talons through the fire, the shield that guards the innocent. I shall seek to wear no crown, nor win any glory. . . .*

That was the oath of the Guardians of the Great Ga'Hoole Tree on the Island of Hoole in the middle of the Sea of Hoolemere.

CHAPTER TWO

A Journey Is Planned

The ember's glow bloomed like an enormous bloodred flower, casting vermilion shadows over the white-feathered faces of the two Barn Owls.

"Coryn," Soren began to speak slowly. "I have been thinking. In the last few days many owls have come to the great tree. They are even calling it the 'Golden Tree' not just because of its golden glow but because a new era has begun since our defeat of the Pure Ones. Word of our library has spread. Owls are on the wing — and are less fearful. They want to know about our chaws. They are especially interested in our weather and navigation chaws." Soren paused and blinked. "What do you say, lad? Shall we have a go of it?" And to himself he thought, *Nothing like a little expedition with the Band to dissolve the gollymopes.*

"What do you mean . . . 'have a go'?" Coryn blinked at Soren. His uncle, although still a handsome owl, had uncountable nicks and marks of battles and from his life as a collier. His beak had long lost its pale tawny glimmer and was now tarnished from his years of plunging into forest fires to retrieve coals. His talons, too, had darkened and grown knobby with fire calluses. The white feathers of his legs were patchy and ash-colored. He looked like a hardened, seasoned owl and yet vigor and gentleness still flowed from him.

"I mean travel, dear lad. Get the lay of the land. See what, exactly, these owls want to learn from us. Besides, it's been so long since any of us have had a good flight — just for fun. Do you know that there is much talk that grog trees, which have been so rare in recent times, are now coming back? There's even rumor of gadfeathers, by Glaux. How lovely to gather with one's old friends in the branches of a grog tree and listen to the sweet tunes of a gadfeather. Ahh, to see old friends again!"

"Mist!" Coryn exclaimed excitedly.

"You call her Mist, but Gylfie and I shall always think of her as Hortense. She must be getting on now, but I long to go to Ambala and seek her out." Soren detected a new sparkle in his nephew's eyes. *Yes, this is it. I must get him out and on the wing. This obsession with his haggish mother is dangerous. Too self-absorbed, an unwholesome indulgence for a king, especially one as intelligent and bold as Coryn.* "How about it?"

"Yes . . ." Coryn said slowly.

"You are worried that kings shouldn't just have fun?" Soren blinked at his nephew.

"Well, I don't want to be thought of as . . ." He hesitated.

"A sporting king?"

"I suppose so, yes."

"But," Soren said eagerly now, "even a king must be curious about how the hard-won peace lies on the land. These are exciting times."

"It is a good plan, Uncle!" Coryn spoke now with genuine enthusiasm. "But we should meet with the Band to discuss it first, don't you think?"

"Yes, of course," Soren agreed. "We'll speak with them immediately and the parliament must be consulted on the morrow. First Black."

"And Otulissa, will she come as well?" Coryn asked. Otulissa, although considered by many a prickly sort with a confidence bordering on arrogance, was a favorite of Coryn's. Otulissa was the first Guardian of Ga'Hoole that Coryn had met. Through some scroomish vision, an odd phenomenon in itself for an owl who was so dedicated to rational thought, Otulissa had been inspired to go to the Beyond. It was there she encountered Coryn and seemed instantly to sense his destiny and that she was part of it. It was Otulissa, the prodigiously talented and knowledge-able Spotted Owl, who first taught Coryn to dive for coals. She claimed no credit, however, for Coryn had a remark-able genius for colliering and in no time had learned to pluck the most challenging of coals from the volcanoes' spume — the bonk ones that many colliers never learned to retrieve.

"I doubt if Otulissa, with her additional responsibili-ties, will be able to accompany us," Coryn said. "But I shall certainly ask her."

Otulissa, an esteemed teacher of the tree, had recently been appointed chief ryb, as her expertise extended over so many of the disciplines — from the literature of the legends to the sciences, including weather interpretation and metals. She hardly had a moment to spare. Nonetheless Soren would go to the hollow where she resided with her old nest-maid snake, Audrey, to ask if she would travel with them. But first he would meet with Gylfie, Twilight, and Digger. And, of course, he would have to explain to Pelli. No doubt Basha, Blythe, and Bell would beg Soren to wait until they had fledged their flight feathers so they might go, too. But they were at least a moon cycle away from fledging, and this was not a trip for young'uns.

Soren was just about to leave the hollow, immensely

pleased with himself for coming up with this idea, when Coryn suddenly said, "Uncle?"

"Yes?"

"What about the ember?"

"The ember? What about it?" Soren asked, slightly bewildered.

"Will it be safe here?"

"I can't imagine a safer place than here in the great tree. We certainly don't want to carry it around with us." He paused and looked steadily at the ember. In a low voice he said, "We do not want to become slaves to the ember. If the legends taught us anything, it was that."

"You are right, Uncle. We are free owls!"

CHAPTER THREE
What About the Ember?

Coryn looked across at the members of the parliament perched on the bow-shaped birch limb. In his head he was searching for the right words to announce this trip. Soren was right. It would be curious to see how peace lay across the owl kingdoms now that the threat of the Pure Ones was gone — or at least greatly diminished. He was interested in not only what he and the Band might learn, but what they might possibly share with the rest of the owl kingdoms now that this menace was gone and every ounce of energy did not have to be devoted to fighting and war. This reminded Coryn of the owls who had arrived at the tree recently and told them of a meeting in Ambala. Coryn coughed slightly and began.

"As most of you know, a small delegation from Ambala arrived three nights ago. They told us of a loose confederation of owls from the Shadow Forest, Silverveil, and, I believe, Tyto that came to meet there. It seems these owls are most interested in weather interpretation, as well as search-and-rescue techniques, and we felt . . ."

Coryn had hardly finished the explanation of the trip he and the Band had planned when there was a great rustling of feathers in the parliament chamber and a half dozen voices began murmuring, "The ember. What about the ember?"

The discussion dragged on with frequent interjections of "What about the ember?"

They're obsessed! thought Soren. And he believed if he had to hear those four words one more time, he would shree as only a Barn Owl could shree.

For perhaps the third time Soren made his argument that there was no safer place for the ember than right here in the tree. It was then suggested that Bubo make another cask for the ember.

"What's wrong with the one ye got?" Bubo, burly Great Horned Owl and chief blacksmith of the tree, growled.

"Is it strong enough, Bubo?" Elyan, a handsome Great Gray Owl and member of the navigation chaw, spoke up.

"Of course, it's strong enough. Fired with the best bonk coals around. Them coals are straight out of Dunmore. Caught on the fly they were, by Ruby over there."

Five volcanoes comprised what the wolves of the Beyond called the Sacred Ring, and the one named Hrath'ghar was the volcano from which Coryn had retrieved the ember. Ruby, a powerful Short-eared Owl known for her extraordinary powers of flight and her near legendary colliering skills, had caught four fantastic bonk coals on a trip back to the Beyond shortly after Coryn had arrived at the tree. "I don't know what more you could ask for!" Bubo fumed. His exceedingly bushy ear tufts twitched, and his eyes showed a touch of rancor. Although most Great Horneds had rather somber plumage composed of dusty browns and dark grays, Bubo's feathers were shot through with deep rusty reds and bronzes. It was almost as if they had taken on the hues of those bonk fires he nurtured. His coloring fit his temperament. Quick to flare, Bubo did not suffer fools gladly. He seemed on the brink now of doing just that as he looked at Elyan, for he suspected that a fool perched across from him.

"Surely the container is not the only security problem." Gemma, a Whiskered Screech, spoke up now.

"What other problems are there?" Bubo asked, feeling that there might be more than one fool in the parliament hollow.

Gemma straightened up and looked down her beak. "As my esteemed late kins-owl, Ezylryb . . ."

Ezylryb? She's comparing herself to Ezylryb! Soren thought.

"...always said, 'Vigilance is its own reward.'" Both Bubo and Soren looked confused. Soren, for one, could not remember Ezylryb ever saying such a thing. "It is my feeling that we not only need a much stronger container but that the coal must be under constant surveillance. A guard must be set up, a dedicated guard, chosen from the most trustworthy Guardians. An elite guard, the — how shall I put it?— Guardians of the Guardians? I am sure Ezylryb ..."

Otulissa blinked her eyes and twisted her head toward Soren.

"With all due respect, Gemma, you're no Ezylryb." The words were not Otulissa's but Bubo's. There was a sharp inhalation of breaths. The owls of the parliament blinked rapidly.

"I'm not sure what you mean by that," Gemma replied huffily.

"I mean *you* are *no* Ezylryb. He wouldn't put up with any of this nonsense about Guardians of Guardians, and some of us being more trustworthy than others —"

"I am sure that all of us here have only one thought in mind: the safety and well-being of the ember," Gemma interrupted. "Ezylryb valued vigilance. I mean, it's not a job that you would want to hand over to nest-maids."

"What!" Soren almost barked. He swiveled his head around. "I've never heard anything so absurd! What in the name of Glaux is not trustworthy about our nest-maid snakes, pray tell? We trust them with our very lives when we are sick or wounded. And you suggest we should not trust them with the ember? I'd wager they are as vigilant as they are skillful in the medical arts. And let us not forget their finely tuned sensibilities. If anything would go awry with the ember, or an ill-intentioned owl approached, it would be the nest-maids to first sound the alarm."

A wizened elderly Northern Saw-whet raised a shaky talon to speak.

"Fleemus has the perch!" Digger shouted. "Let the good owl speak."

Fleemus, the doctor and healer of the great tree, lifted an arthritic wing. "When I first arrived at this great tree many years ago, there was much of which to be fearful. There were the Pure Ones, as well as those thugs from St. Aggie's — with whom Soren and Gylfie were all too well-acquainted. When I began my practice here in the tree, only matron and her small contingent of nurse owls were trained as field medics for battle. Since that time, however, we have an entire new guild of nest-maid snakes whose sole focus is the medical arts. If you can't trust a nest-maid snake, you can't trust anyone." He paused. Then in a small, creaky voice, he added, "I think all this talk about security is nonsense, nothing more than a pile of racdrops." He muttered something in a strange language.

"What was that?" Gemma asked. "What did you just say?"

"Krakish, from the Northern Kingdoms from which both your old kins-owl Ezylryb and I came. Indeed, it was the language of the famous sagas of the Northern Kingdoms, *The History of the Wars of the Ice Claws* by Lyze of Kiel."

"And what does this Lyze of Kiel have to say?" Gemma lifted her beak in a most haughty manner.

"Fyrndronken nyghot ig fyrnsfris."

"And for those of us not fluent in Krakish?" Gemma pressed. A sneer tinged her words.

"We have nothing to fear except fear itself," Fleemus replied. There was a murmuring among the owls. Soren and Gylfie were watching Gemma carefully. They sensed what was about to happen.

"And who is this so-called historian? 'Lyze of Kiel' you called him?" She could barely contain the contempt in her voice, and had Soren and Gylfie not known what the answer to her question was, their gizzards would have twitched in sympathy for old Fleemus.

"Why, Gemma," Fleemus said with a wicked sparkle suddenly infusing his rheumy old eyes. "Lyze of Kiel? You don't know him? Why, he's your old kins-owl, Ezylryb. He wrote these histories after the Ice Talon Wars ended, and before he came to the great tree. He spent years with Octavia at the Glauxian Brothers retreat on their island in the Bitter Sea, writing under the pen name Lyze of Kiel. Invert the letters and they spell Ezyl. And, as we all know, Ezyl, our dear departed ryb, came from the Bay of Kiel in the Everwinter Sea."

"Apparently not all of us," someone whispered as Gemma wilfed to half her size.

Soren winked at Gylfie and both the owls silently saluted the dear old healer who, many years after Ezylryb, had come from that same Glauxian retreat. Otulissa now turned to Gemma. "The books are in the library and are part of my standard curriculum for the young'uns, if you'd care to read them."

Several owls, perhaps a dozen, began to squabble again. The words "ember security," "tree vigilance," and "island protection" threaded through the air. Soren exchanged a quick glance with Coryn. The parliament seemed evenly divided. There were Fleemus and the Band in addition to Otulissa; Soren's sister, Eglantine; Ruby; Martin—in short, the renowned and remarkable Chaw of Chaws, a group that had no equal in terms of fighting skills, felt that the ember needed no special guard. The rest of the parliament thought otherwise. These ten owls seemed stunned by this new obsession with security and fear concerning the ember. Soren in particular wondered if it had been a mistake that they had not read the ancient legends aloud to the entire parliament. But Otulissa had given three extensive lectures on them and the "complicated goodness," as she had called it, of the ember. *Perhaps,* Soren thought, *she should have called it complicated "dangers" rather than "goodness."* But she had certainly warned of the pitfalls of overreliance on the ember's magic.

"Here! here!" Coryn flapped his wings and swooped off his perch. He flew up to Gemma and Elyan, who were the most obstreperous of all the owls, and glared at them. The hollow fell silent. "I shall not have you all talking at once. Dissent is welcome in this hollow, but I am hearing insults as well. You are talking about protecting something, the ember that many of you feel will somehow become vulnerable if I leave the great tree on this flight. I do not want you to feel uncomfortable in my absence. So, if it will make you feel better, yes, protect it. But there is no one owl or creature in this tree who is more trustworthy than another. The notion of an inner group of Guardians — Guardians of Guardians — is contrary to all that we value. If there is to be a watch — and I prefer to call it a watch, not a guard — it must have a representative from every chaw and each guild of the nest-maid snakes — those of the harp, the weavers, the lace-makers, the new medical and nursing guild, and so on."

"And how shall this ... this ... watch be chosen?" Gemma asked.

Coryn blinked. "The ember is in my hollow. I have spent more time in its presence than any other living creature. I think that it is only appropriate that I appoint those who will be perching in my hollow." Soren was proud of Coryn's quick and firm response. Coryn paused. "Now listen to me, owls, and listen hard." He blinked. There was a new sternness in his voice that went beyond the firmness they had just heard. Was it threatening? Some of the owls wilfed a bit. "When I first came here, I said to you that I had survived the ordeal of my upbringing with Nyra because I believed in the legends, the truths of courage and loyalty and of goodness and mercy. Those, indeed, were the truths of the popular legends that you all listened to as young'uns. The even older legends of which you have heard Otulissa speak held other truths. And one of them was that we must not become slaves of the ember. Fear enslaves. Remember that. And I command that the ancient legends, the ones that Ezylryb directed me to read with Soren, now be placed in the library and read by all of you. If you read these legends, you will learn respect and not fear. With knowledge comes freedom — freedom to think, freedom to reason. The ember and its magic have nothing to do with thinking and that is perhaps why it can be so dangerous."

No one said another word as the owls flew out of the hollow.

CHAPTER FOUR
The Band Takes Flight

The Band had gathered in Coryn's hollow to discuss the "security of the ember."

"No! It's out of the question. I don't want to be on some council for guarding this thing." Otulissa tossed her head at the ember, which did seem to spit a few sparks in reponse to her disparaging tone. "I have too much to do. You know that new bunch in training for colliering is a feisty group. Great Glaux, Fritha is always just winging off, chasing embers that she has no business going after. She has no sense of playing her ground position, which is essentially what we rely on the Pygmy Owls for. And then, of course, there are my chores in the library. No, I will not 'ember-sit' or whatever you call it."

"Well, I'd appoint Eglantine, but she's my aunt and I'm afraid that wouldn't appear, well . . . quite proper," Coryn replied.

"What about Audrey? You could do without her for a bit, couldn't you, Otulissa?" Soren asked.

"Audrey? Well, I suppose so. Audrey might even enjoy it. She might consider it an honor — bless her simple heart."

"Not so with Octavia," Gylfie said.

"Oh, Great Glaux," Otulissa churred. "Octavia would think the whole thing totally yoicks."

"Madame Plonk?" Digger offered.

"Now that's an interesting idea. It might appeal to Madame Plonk." Madame Plonk was the great singer of the tree, quite vain about many things, and the group thought it might be just her thing to serve on this ember watch.

It did not take Coryn long to come up with his suggested list for the watch. Ultimately, it was composed of twenty owls, some members of parliament like Gemma, Elyan, and Yeena, a Barn Owl, a half dozen nest-maid snakes, and the rest pulled from the various chaws. It was a well-balanced group in everyone's estimation. There were no hurt feelings, and no one, aside from Otulissa, refused to serve.

And so at First Black, the young king and the Band rose in the night on a snappish wind that swirled down from the north, and headed out across the Sea of Hoolemere on a course toward Ambala. The shadows of the five owls were printed against the almost full-shine moon with Coryn flying in the lead position, flanked on one side by Soren and on the other by Twilight. Gylfie flew just behind Twilight's starboard wing, her favorite position as navigator, for she was sucked along effortlessly by the powerful Great Gray's forward thrust and could concentrate on the stars rather than flying. Digger brought up the rear.

"Two points south by southeast of the bottom star, port talon of the Golden Talons," Gylfie called out.

Soren felt his gizzard sing. How long ago it had been since he and Gylfie had flown as young'uns in those early navigation practices with Strix Struma? One of her favorite exercises was for them to trace with their wing tips the outline of the Golden Talons constellation, which shone in the winter sky at its brightest just this time of year. It seemed like a lifetime ago. Now here was Gylfie, the head of the navigation chaw and regarded as one of the most brilliant celestial navigators in the kingdoms of owls.

But in owl years they weren't that old. Yes, older than they were back then, but still strong and fit. Soren knew they must show the rest of the owl world their wonderful king and bring with them the skills and knowledge that they had learned at the great tree. Coryn was right. Knowledge was freedom and no one could be enslaved if they dared to really think. If good things came out of this flight through the owl kingdoms they would be to dispel the myth of the ember and to help owls believe in themselves and their own power of thought. They would learn what could be accomplished through the disciplines that had been so highly developed at the great tree: colliering, navigating by the stars, and the science of interpreting weather. Soren had a name for all of this knowledge and it had nothing to do with magic. He called it the "glories of common sense."

A seagull flew up to them. "Hey, Twilight!"

"Sammy!" Twilight exclaimed. "Haven't seen you in an age."

"Gotta great wet poop joke for you," the seagull said.

"Oh, dear! Should I close my ear slits?" Gylfie asked.

"Oh, sure!" Twilight flicked his head toward the little Elf Owl. "We know how delicate you are! Who told that joke to that snooty great blue heron back in Silverveil and nearly got a fish thrown in her face?" Twilight turned his head to the seagull. "So what's the joke, Sammy?"

"What's the difference between a wet pooper and a pellet yarper?"

The Band looked at one another and exchanged glances. "I don't know. I give up," Twilight said.

The seagull had already started to laugh at his own

joke and could hardly finish it. "It's a matter of splatter!" the seagull screamed. He was now completely convulsed with laughter and ricocheted off the edge of a thermal draft into a cold trough and was gone.

"Glaux, he barely made it to the punch line!" Gylfie exclaimed.

They were all laughing now. *Lucky Otulissa isn't here,* Soren thought. She did not like what she termed "elimination humor." She always became very upset when they were out on weather-interpretation chaws and encountered seagulls, who were the coarsest of birds. But this rough humor was just what Coryn needed. He needed to get away — away from the tree, away from the squabbling parliament, and yes, away from the ember. Maybe in the good company of the Band he would relax, join in their easy, joyful camaraderie, and those terrible thoughts that haunted him would pass. If they had never read the legends, Soren had wondered lately, would Coryn have become so fixated on his past? Perhaps even more interesting, Soren wondered if Coryn had ever had any carefree days when he was being raised by Nyra. Did he ever have a friend as a young'un? Coryn had once mentioned an owl — a Sooty named Phillip. But he never wanted to talk about Phillip. It seemed to make him extremely sad. The Pure Ones were known to discriminate against any owl who was not a *Tyto alba*. Sooties — although a kind of Barn Owl — occupied the lowest perch in the world of the Pure Ones. So this Phillip's life was bound to have been a hard one.

Soren's life had not been an easy one, either, after his fall from the family hollow in the forest of Tyto. But it would have been unspeakably worse if he had not met up with Gylfie, Twilight, and Digger. The Band had become his family when he had none. They had become one another's reasons for living, flying on through obstacle after obstacle to reach the tree so long ago. In truth, Soren had learned as much from Digger, Gylfie, and Twilight as from any book. And he must not forget Ezylryb. Just as there was a Chaw of Chaws — the Band, plus Otulissa, Martin, Ruby, and Eglantine — there was also a ryb of rybs: Ezylryb.

CHAPTER FIVE
Tell It! Tell It!

A contrary wind had risen, and holding the course for Ambala was tiring after their crossing of the Hoolemere Sea. Dawn was approaching and so the five owls decided to head for Silverveil, one of the most delightful forests in all the owl kingdoms, with its lush meadows sprinkled with wildflowers in the summer and its forests of old and stately trees. Silverveil was the place where Coryn had first begun to understand what the color green really was. His entire childhood until the time he had escaped from Nyra and the Pure Ones had been spent in the barren, rocky scrub landscape of the canyonlands, which were bereft of anything resembling a tree, let alone green leaves or spruce or pine needles.

Within the forest of Silverveil, there was a pocket of green splendor called Blythewold that was as pretty as any place on Earth. Soren and Pelli had named one of their daughters Blythe after this place. And it was here that Coryn had lived for a long time before summoning his courage to leave for the Beyond. It was a place replete with memories — some good, some bad. It was a scroomish place where he had been haunted by the spirit of his father, Kludd, but also where he had heard for the first time some of the better-known legends of Ga'Hoole. He had eavesdropped on parents telling these stories at good-light time to their hatchlings before they went to sleep. While in the forest, Coryn had lived hidden in the stump of a tree in a day-for-night world because too often he had been mistaken for his terrible mother.

"Winter is finally upon us, I think," Soren said as they lighted down on a wildly waving branch of a large fir tree. Soren was partial to fir trees. They formed part of his first memories. Like Coryn's, some of these memories were good and some were bad. But it was the good ones that he tried to concentrate on. Those times in the old family hollow of the fir tree in the forest of Tyto where he had first heard his father tell the stories of Ga'Hoole. Little did he know then that the great tree was a real place. And how vividly he remembered what his father had said to his brother, Kludd, when Kludd had asked him if the legends were true. "A legend, Kludd," his father had replied, "is a story that you begin to feel in your gizzard, which over time becomes true in your heart." But would his father ever have believed that there really was an island called Hoole, where the Great Ga'Hoole Tree did, indeed, grow? Could he ever have imagined that Soren would become a Guardian and that his own grandson, Coryn, son of Kludd, would become king? And would he have believed that Kludd had pushed Soren from the nest, attempting to murder him as part of his own rites of initiation into the brutal gang of owls called the Pure Ones? Soren shook the past from his mind.

It had begun to snow. "If I know fir trees, there will be a nice roomy hollow, dry and sweet-smelling," Soren looked up, "oh, I'd say about a third of the way from the top on the lee side of the trunk."

And there was. The five owls crowded in. "I'm starved!" Twilight announced. "This place is hopping with rabbits."

"Mmmmm!" Digger, Gylfie, and Soren all smacked their beaks in anticipation. Gylfie turned to Coryn. "Not up for a rabbit?" she asked.

"Well, rabbits are fine. Just don't go after one that has a white mark on its forehead."

"Why?" Twilight blinked.

"It's a long story," Coryn said.

"This is a morning for long stories," Soren said as he watched the thickening swirls of snow outside the hollow.

"Not on an empty gizzard, it isn't!" Twilight boomed. "Let's get hunting."

"I'll go with you," Coryn said.

"Good idea. I wouldn't want to grab the wrong rabbit."

Twilight and Coryn had been tracking a large gray rabbit when Coryn suddenly picked up soft mewling noises. "Grosnik!" he hissed.

"Oh, for the love of Glaux! Are you sure, Coryn?"

"I heard the babies," Coryn whispered. Barn Owls were known for their extraordinary hearing abilities, which allowed them to detect the subtlest of sounds.

"And no parent?" Twilight asked.

"No. Look — there's the den down there under that tree stump. I would have definitely picked up the parent's heartbeat if there was one in there."

Among owls it was strictly forbidden to eat baby animals or to kill a parent if there was only one parent, thus leaving the babies orphaned. Of course, this was not always known to the hunter and many small animals had been orphaned when owls had unwittingly preyed upon their parents. But the circumstances here were clear. These babies, at least four, Coryn thought, would have been orphaned.

Twilight sighed. "It's funny, once you get your gizzard set on something, you can almost taste it before your first bite and you want nothing else. Vole seems so boring to me right now."

"Well, as you said, there are lots of rabbits around here."

"Yeah, they can't all have babies, or white marks on their forehead . . . I hope!"

"No, believe me," Coryn said, "there was only one rabbit like that."

"What was its name?"

"He had no name."

"No name? What made that rabbit so special?"

"He just was. Don't worry about it. It all happened long ago, in the Shadow Forest. Not here. I'm just always really careful when I go out rabbit hunting to check to see if my prey has that mark. He called himself a mystic. You know, he could see things that other creatures couldn't — sort of like Soren has starsight and I can read the flames of a fire. Well, this rabbit could read things in spiderwebs."

"You gotta be kidding!" Twilight exclaimed.

"No, not at all." Coryn paused. "My visions are mostly about the present but the rabbit had bits and pieces of the past, the present, and the future. You see . . ." Coryn was about to explain what the rabbit actually saw. "There's one now!"

"Him? The one with the mark?"

"No!"

A large fluffy white rabbit darted under the bank of a creek. Amid the swirling snow, he appeared like a solid sphere hurtling across the frozen bed of the creek. Twilight was on him in a flash. Coryn admired the speed with which the Great Gray killed. No matter what the wind direction was, it never offset his kill angle and he always managed to plunge his talons directly into the brain of the animal so that it was an instant, nearly pain-less death.

"That is one beautiful rabbit!" Digger exclaimed as Twilight and Coryn returned to the hollow. It was custom-ary among owls that whoever made the kill got the first choice of meat, or "firsts" as it was often called. Undoubtedly, Twilight would go for a haunch, for that was usually the meatiest on a rabbit. Soren, however, looked at the rabbit and said, "Hold on a second, Twilight. Before you get your firsts, don't you think we should skin this rabbit properly? This is a beautiful pelt. Trader Mags came by last moon cycle with a pelt like this torn from a robe."

"One of the Others' robes?" Digger asked.

"Yes, of course. And she sold it to Madame Plonk for Glaux knows what. The piece was moth-eaten and not nearly as glistening white as this pelt," Soren said.

"Are you suggesting that we try to best Trader Mags at her own game?" Gylfie asked.

"I'm just saying that the new sewing guild the nest-maid snakes formed might be happy to get something like this. Or maybe we should just keep it for ourselves. Divide it up. Everyone could have a piece for their hollow."

"Oh, for Glaux's sake, if you're going to skin it, skin it. I'm famished," Twilight roared.

"Let's skin it," Coryn said.

And so they did. As they sat enjoying the rabbit, which was unusually plump for this time of year, Soren suddenly said, "Do any of you remember that time — oh, we were much younger than young Coryn here — when we snuck out of the tree?"

"We snuck out at least a hundred times," Gylfie said. "Which time?"

"You snuck out?" Coryn blinked.

"Of course we did," Digger replied.

"Did you get into trouble?" Coryn asked.

"Sometimes," Soren said.

"Was it worth it?"

"Always!" the Band roared in unison.

"Well, what time was this one?" Coryn turned to Soren.

Soren wiped the blood from his beak. "Well, it was right after a visit from Trader Mags and we had this idea — we were always fascinated about the Others —"

"Who isn't?" Coryn asked.

"Anyhow," Soren continued. "We had this idea that we would go find a new castle, or church, or — I don't know — one of those stone hollows that the Others built, but one that Trader Mags hadn't scavenged yet for all the goodies. We were going to get rich. I guess that was the main idea. Going to start our own business. I mean, we were young. We thought it would be fun going around selling things or swapping them."

"Otulissa said that the idea was stupid and that noble owls weren't meant for business," Gylfie said. "Remember? That was why she wouldn't come with us. She said it was vulgar."

"That is soooo Otulissa!" Digger said.

"It probably *was* common, but it would have been fun," Gylfie said.

"Well, did you go?" Coryn asked.

"Oh, we did!" Soren said. "We flew first to Tyto thinking that if there were any undiscovered Others' ruins they might be there. But we didn't find any. Then . . . I don't know whose idea it was to head to the Shadow Forest . . ."

"Mine!" Twilight chimed in. "I had dimly remembered something from my very youngest days. You realize, Coryn, that I was orphaned very young. Never knew my parents."

I should have been so lucky, Coryn thought.

"Had to teach myself everything. Orphan School of Tough Learning is what I call it. For me, the great tree was more of a finishing school than anything else."

"If that's not a pile of racdrops, I don't know what is!" Digger blinked.

"Give it a blow, Twilight. Finishing school, my talon." Gylfie stomped her tiny talons on the floor of the hollow.

"Anyway," Soren continued, "we decided to go to the Shadow Forest. And we did find a ruin. There were no jewels, no great tapestries like the ones Trader Mags salvages scraps from, no paintings. There was something much more precious."

"What was that?"

"Bess," Gylfie said quietly.

"Bess?" Coryn asked.

"Yes, Bess — the daughter of Grimble!" There were tears now in both Soren's and Gyfie's eyes.

"And who is Grimble?" Coryn asked.

"Was," Gylfie corrected, and wiped away a tear with her wing tip. "You see, Coryn, Grimble taught us to fly. It was because of Grimble that Soren and I were able to escape St. Aggie's."

Soren continued. "Grimble was killed when the Ablah General discovered him helping us to escape. There was a terrific fight. Grimble kept yelling, 'Fly! Fly! Now's your chance!' I looked back and saw him bleeding on the ground, a wing half torn off."

"And did he die?" Coryn asked.

"Oh, he died all right. But his bones brought Bess and us together."

"His bones!" Coryn blinked. "Is this a scroom story?"

"In a way," Gylfie said softly. "But it was because we had snuck out to look for precious things that we found Bess in that ruin. It was several moon cycles after her father had finally died. She would have rescued him if she could have. But she couldn't, so she did the next best thing and brought his bones to this secret place."

"Secret place!" Coryn was nearly jumping out of his feathers. "Tell me the story, please." *A child desperate to rescue a parent! How different from me. Would I ever dare rescue my mum, or . . . ? Would I dare seek out my da's bones?*

A shadow seemed to steal across Soren's gizzard, sending a deep chill through his hollow bones. "I can remember her words almost exactly." Soren sighed.

"Tell it! Tell it!"

"Yes, you tell it, Soren," Gylfie said. Soren was the best storyteller of all. It was Soren's telling of the legends when he and Gylfie had been thrown into the moon-blaze chamber in St. Aggie's that had saved them from being moon blinked. There was a passion in his telling of stories that made the words take on new and deeper meanings. But it wasn't simply a story he would be telling Coryn. Soren would be telling him of a secret place that only a very few owls in the great tree knew about, only the Band, Otulissa, Ezylryb, and Strix Struma, and, yes, two nest-maid snakes — Octavia and Mrs. Plithiver. They called it the Palace of Mists.

CHAPTER SIX
Bess of the Chimes

We had taken off during the milkberry harvest festival — always a good time to sneak out," Soren began. "You know how all those older owls get tipsy on the milkberry wine and berry mead. And then there is all the dancing and singing that can go on for three days or more. We knew that we wouldn't be missed. No one paid much attention to young owls at these times, especially back then. We had hardly been at the tree a year, maybe thirteen moon cycles at the most, when we got this notion of getting rich. Beating old Trader Mags at her own game, as Gylfie said. Otulissa would have nothing to do with it. It was raining that night as well she argued. So, why be out when there was so much frolic going on in the great hollow of the tree?"

"Yes, but the winds were terrific," Twilight said. "Rain or no rain, the winds were with us from behind. So we flew fast."

"As I recall, " Digger offered, "we made Cape Glaux by daybreak."

"But where would you even start looking for a ruin — an undiscovered one?" Coryn asked.

Soren blinked and began to speak in his thoughtful way. "Good question. We were smart enough not to go to Silverveil. We knew Trader Mags had discovered all the ruins there. But the one place that had never really been explored was part of the Shadow Forest. It's so dense with trees that there was not much space for the Others to build their stone hollows. We were young and impulsive, and although we had once been attacked by crows, we promised ourselves that we would be more vigilant this time. So we decided to go out and hunt during the morning hours but always together and then at night to go off separately to cover as much of the forest as possible in search of a ruin."

Coryn listened with rapt attention. What an adventure! A treasure hunt instead of a battle. Jewels instead of blood. And most of all, friendship. Daring young owls sneaking off from the great tree together on a quest.

"By the end of the second day, we had found nothing and we knew time was getting short. We would have to get back to the tree. But that night we went out once more separately and Gylfie . . ." Soren paused. "Well, Gylfie, you should tell this part."

Gylfie ran her beak through her primaries before she began her part of the story. "There is a place in the Shadow Forest where, if you fly high enough and are observant, you will notice the forest seems to dip down into a bowl. If you look closer, you will see the silvery ropes of a waterfall cascading from a great height into the bowl. I saw the falls sending up great plumes of swirling mist. I spiraled down and flew closer. Veils of mist were suspended in the air. The entire valley seemed to be neither quite of land or sky but hanging between the two. I began to see shapes in the mist as one sees shapes in the clouds. But then I slowly realized that these were not mere illusions or figments of my imagination. What I was seeing was real and made of stone. I flew back to the place we were to meet up if we found anything.

"When we all flew there together, the mist was so thick you couldn't see a thing. It was like a curtain hanging across the valley," Gylfie continued. "The rest of the Band thought I had experienced some sort of gizzard dream. There wasn't a stone visible. But suddenly, a sharp rogue wind tore through the curtain of mist like a knife. Four beautiful stone spires pierced the night. And that's when Soren heard the chimes."

"Chimes!" Coryn exclaimed. It all sounded so mysterious, so beautiful. "What was it?"

"I thought it was battle gear clanking in the night," Twilight said.

"Only you, Twilight, would think that!" Digger sighed.

"But was it chimes? A bell tolling?" Coryn asked.

"In a sense," Soren spoke softly.

Coryn felt a shiver pass through him. *This* was *going to be a scroom story*, he thought.

"We had fetched up just beneath one of the stone towers in a silverdrop pine. It took me about three seconds to identify the sound. It was a Boreal Owl! You know how the call of those owls often sounds like chimes in the night? Well, Boreals believe that if a Boreal dies in a bell tower beneath the clapper of a bell, then its scroom will go straight to glaumora. Or at least that was the tale that our friend Grimble told us."

"You mean," said Coryn, now aghast, "that it was a dying owl making this beautiful chiming noise?"

"It was not a dying owl but the sound was very mournful." Gylfie sighed. Her wings seemed to quiver at the memory of it all.

"And desperate," added Soren. "We decided we should go to her."

"Her? It was a female?" Coryn asked.

"We were pretty sure it was a female. So," Soren

continued, "we took off and flew toward the spire from which the sounds were coming. As we drew nearer, the sounds became louder — as Gylfie said the most mournful yet beautiful sounds any of us had ever heard.

"A strange sight greeted us as we lighted down on the windowsill of the bell tower," Soren continued. "There was a large bell that hung in the tower and from within it came the chimelike sounds mixed with the wing beats of an owl. On the stone floor were the bleached bones of another owl, one long dead."

Coryn felt as if the line between past and present were blurring. It was as if he were actually living within the story; it was as real to him as it was to the Band. Soren's storytelling voice slid through the dim light of the hollow as smoothly as the liquid ribbon of a river flows toward the sea. Coryn felt its current.

"We were perched on the window ledge of the bell tower," Soren said. "Now, we had all experienced scroomish, peculiar things in our days. Things that stilled our gizzards and sent quivers through our bones, but this was one of the strangest situations ever. From the bell we heard a beautiful song, a song that seemed to be made of silver. I cannot sing it but the words were so lovely."

"What were the words?" Coryn pressed.

"I hope I can remember. Say them with me." Soren looked at Gylfie, Twilight, and Digger. The four owls began to recite the song.

> I am the chimes in the night,
> the sound within the wind.
> I am the tolling of glaumora
> for the souls of long-lost kin.
> I shall sing you to the stars,
> where your scroom shall finally rest
> 'neath the great bell of the sky
> in a tower of cloudy crests. . . .

"When the song in the bell finished," Gylfie said, "a beautiful owl flew from the bell and lighted down."

"I'll never forget that first glimpse of her." Soren shut his eyes. "She was the color of tree bark with lighter brown and creamy streaks. Her face was grayish-white with flares of small white feathers radiating out from her eyes. Her wings had five rows of white spots. And on top of her head there was a starry spray of small white feathered dots. The thought burst in my head and Gylfie's, too. She looked exactly like her father, Grimble!"

"Grimble, the owl who helped you escape St. Aggie's?" Coryn whispered excitedly.

"The very one!" Soren replied. "She was not young. I didn't need to ask her her name. I knew immediately she was Bess, Grimble's favorite daughter. She was astonished that we knew who she was. Then she looked down at the bones at her feet. 'And those are the bones of Grimble,' I said. I knew this in my gizzard as surely as I had ever known anything in my life."

Gylfie continued the story. "We told Bess how we had come to know her father at St. Aggie's and how he had saved our lives by teaching us how to fly and how we also knew that Bess was his favorite daughter." Gylfie paused before going on with the story. "Bess could hardly believe this, for she thought her father had abandoned them all. So we explained how he didn't want to stay with the St. Aggie's owls but they threatened to kill her and her mum and the rest of her brothers and sisters if he did not remain."

"Bess blinked," Soren said. His own eyes misted with the memory. "And two big tears rolled from her bright yellow eyes. 'That explains it,' she said. 'We thought he had vanished. That we were nothing to him.'"

Soren shut his eyes tight now and began to speak forcefully, as if he were trying to remember something very exactly. "But we told her that her father had courage in a place that bred cowards. That he had a nobility as great as any Guardian of Ga'Hoole's. And when we asked her how his bones had come to be in this place, she told us that the eagles Streak and Zan had brought them to the family. But that she had brought them to this place for she believed in the old tales her father had told."

Digger now spoke. "The rest of her family had warned her that she would have to go as far as Silverveil to find a bell tower. But she had found this place. And she liked it because it was so hidden in the valley, and the roar of the waterfalls was like a kind of music to her. She said that in many ways it made her think that this was what glaumora must be like and that is why she sang every day to her father. She said that she hoped he was in glaumora and that his business on Earth was finished so that he would not haunt the Earth and the lower air as a scroom."

"But," Soren said, "even though her father had long gone to glaumora, it was almost as if Bess was a scroom, as if *her* business was not finished."

Coryn felt a chill pass through his gizzard. Was his own mother, Nyra, still alive, or was she a scroom? And if she was a scroom, what business had she left unfinished?

CHAPTER SEVEN

The Palace of Mists

"But what was this place where Bess mourned?" Coryn asked. "A castle? Was there gold and silver and the kinds of things that Trader Mags looks for?"

"There was certainly some of that but there was something much more valuable," Soren answered.

"What?" Coryn asked.

"Books and maps." Digger's eyes began to sparkle. "Not just one library but many. Bess said these stone hollows were a university, a place of learning. But she called it a palace. The Palace of Mists."

Digger, like many Burrowing Owls, was a great appreciator of built spaces. As his species name suggested, he was expert in excavating underground tunnels and hollows and creating nests where other birds might not dream of living. He admired the way the stones of the university had been hewn to fit together perfectly and how the entire structure was tucked neatly behind the scrim of mist from the waterfall.

"The Palace of Mists." Coryn repeated the words dreamily.

"Yes, and just imagine, Coryn!" Excitement stirred Digger's normally even, slow speech. "The face of the waterfall formed the rear wall of this palace. And there were four spires, each a bell tower but not one of the four bells had a clapper."

"I bet Bubo could have made one," Coryn said.

"Bess didn't want one," Soren replied. "We were the first owls who ever came there, and she said she liked her secret place and that she needed no clapper to sing her da to glaumora. I'll never forget her words. She said, 'I am the chimes. I am the clapper.' And I do believe had there been no bell she would have become that as well. She is an extraordinary owl, one of vast intelligence."

"Is?" Coryn blurted out. "She still lives?"

"Oh, most definitely." Soren paused and lowered his voice. "You must understand, Coryn, Bess is the best-kept secret in the owl kingdom. When we left Bess that first time, we vowed to tell only three other owls: Otulissa, Ezylryb, and Strix Struma."

"And it was hard enough getting her to agree to that! Believe me!" Twilight said. "But tell Coryn about the stone Others."

Coryn was speechless, his eyes wide.

"Ah, yes, the stone Others," Soren replied. "Bess asked us if we would like a tour of the university. So we followed her in a spiraling flight down from the bell tower, winding in and out of the pillars of a garden where there were stone pictures."

"Stone pictures?" Coryn asked.

"Yeah, you've seen some of those scraps of paintings of Others that Mags brings around, haven't you?" Twilight asked.

"Sure."

"Well, this was sort of the same thing but cut in stone," Twilight replied. "Some were of animals, and there was even a strange-looking bird. And some of the stone figures were of the Others, but they might be missing a head, or a head might be missing a body."

"What in the world?" Coryn gasped. "Were they once alive?"

"Oh, no. It was part of the Others' art, like the paintings."

"But that wasn't the most interesting thing at all," Gylfie said.

"Sounds pretty interesting to me," Coryn replied.

"There were these maps," Soren said. "Maps like we'd never seen before."

"What do you mean?" Coryn asked. A pale lavender light began to suffuse the hollow. Lavender was the prelude of twilight and soon it would be First Black. They had told and listened to stories of Bess through an entire day. Coryn almost wished to stay the sun and fend off the night — a most un-owlish response. Owls lived for darkness, for the black pierced by a sliver of moon, or perhaps the silver disc of a full-shine floating eerily just above a horizon. But now he wanted not the darkness, not the silver, not the joys of flight through a long night, but to remain in the hollow of this fir tree reliving this fantastic tale of discovery, grief, mystery, and riches that were neither jewels nor gold.

"These maps," Soren continued, "were not ones of the owl kingdoms. There was no Sea of Hoolemere, no Everwinter Sea. No Northern Kingdoms. No Southern Kingdoms. So I asked Bess, 'Where are the kingdoms of owls?'"

"And what did she say?" Coryn tipped forward.

"She said they were maps of elsewhere and beyond," Soren said softly.

"It was even beyond our Beyond! We called it The Elsewhere," Digger whispered. The white feathers that streaked across the Burrowing Owl's brow seemed to intensify Digger's penetrating gaze. It was as if he were imagining this place.

Coryn was astonished. He was trying to take it all in.

"You mean there is a place that is not here? Not in this owl world? It's like . . ." Coryn looked out of the fir tree hollow and tipped his head toward the sky.

"Yes," Gylfie said. "And even the stars look different there — the constellations are different. One rarely sees the Golden Talons or the Little or the Big Raccoon. It's just a different world. It's The Elsewhere."

"Have you ever been there?" He looked first at Soren and then to each of the other Band members. They all shook their heads.

"But Bess knows the way there even though the stars are different," Gylfie said. She shook her head in wonder. "Bess is so very smart."

"That is why we call her 'the Knower,'" Soren said.

By the time Soren had finished the story of Bess and the Palace of Mists, it was night. The wind had shifted, so they set out on a course for Ambala. But they did not make much progress, for they were tired and shortly after midnight the wind shifted once again and became a fierce headwind with driving rain replacing the swirls of snow.

"No use fighting this," Twilight called out to the rest. If Twilight said it was too much — beating into this wind — the rest of the Band were quick to agree, for the Great Gray was the largest of them all and possessed the most wing power. They found an ancient cedar with a good-size hollow. The rain made the pungent scent of the tree even sharper.

"I can't say cedar is my fragrance of choice," Gylfie sniffed, but within two seconds she had fallen asleep.

All of the owls were soon asleep except for Coryn. For him sleep seemed beyond reason. "The Knower," Coryn repeated softly. He began to think deeply about Bess, the Knower.

His mind whirled with notions about Bess and this place dedicated entirely to learning, with many libraries. The Band had said they had never seen such maps and star charts. Coryn knew that the Others were thought to have been very advanced, but not so advanced as these stories of the Palace of Mists seemed to suggest. From the stonework to the star charts it seemed beyond belief, almost magical. Coryn's eyes began to droop. His last thought was, *Magic, or nachtmagen?*

Then Coryn began dreaming of stone gardens with the fragments of the Others and stone animals, and the strange-looking stone bird that Soren had described. In his sleep he saw a head. It was the head of the strange bird. But no, not just any strange bird — Kreeth!

He woke up immediately. "Why would I ever dream of Kreeth?" he whispered to himself. Kreeth, the infamous hagsfiend of the legends, was long dead. Surely if the strange stone bird looked like Kreeth, the Band would have said something. Although they had not known about the hagsfiends of the legends when they had first gone to the Palace of Mists, they would have remembered now. *This is totally irrational!* Coryn thought to himself.

Kreeth was a hagsfiend through and through, but she called herself by all sorts of other names — a philosopher, an experimenter, a scientist. It wasn't, however, science she practiced. It was nachtmagen. Although he had begun to suspect that beneath the plumage of a Barn Owl his mother might be a hagsfiend herself, a grotesque thought occurred to him again — that Nyra might be even worse than haggish. She might be some descendant of a remnant of Kreeth's experiments with nachtmagen. It was all too frightening to imagine. Coryn blinked. But imagine he must. He was a king, a leader. He must lead! And to lead was to imagine boldly.

He looked at the Band sleeping soundly around him. Outside the sun was high in the sky. He must go. He must risk being mobbed by crows. He must find out the truth about his mother. Hagsfiends were thought to have become extinct sometime long after King Hoole had retrieved the ember. And yet shadows of hagsfiends much less potent still lingered. And was that not what

made the ember so puzzling? For with all its many blessings, there was always the lurking fear that, with the good
magen, nachtmagen could return and real hagsfiends
could slip back through what Otulissa called the ether
veil of the owl universe. The ether was a windless layer of
air in the upper regions of the sky that enveloped the
entire universe of owls. The ancients believed that infini-
tesimally small tears in this layer could permit the
intrusion of alien matter such as nachtmagen, the magic
of hagsfiends. The ember could seal up these tears as well
as open them. And if the ember came into the possession
of a bad owl, or graymalkin as they were sometimes called,
the ether could be ripped to shreds.

Coryn was fairly sure that no such thing had happened
to the ether veil — yet. According to the legends, Kreeth
had died. But were all her kind extinct? Like the Others?
Perhaps not, if Nyra lived. Coryn knew what he had to do.
He had to go to the Shadow Forest. However he did not
need to see Bess. The Knower would not know what he
needed to know. There was, however, a rabbit who might.
And he needed to find that rabbit. He quietly stepped to
the rim of the hollow. He looked back at the Band. *They're
just going to have to understand,* he thought, and spreading his
wings, he took off.

CHAPTER EIGHT

Otulissa Perplexed

"Can you feel it, Mrs. Plithiver?" Octavia asked. The elderly nest-maid snake was coiled on an upper limb of the Great Ga'Hoole Tree.

"Yes, they're flying in unison. I can feel the wing beats."

And indeed a surge of vibrations rolled up through the tree. The slender branch upon which they had arranged themselves was almost like a tuning fork, at least for nest-maid snakes. These snakes had extremely refined sensibilities and despite their blindness, they could pick up on the subtlest atmospheric pressure changes, sounds, wind shifts, even the feelings and moods of those around them. Octavia, a snake of ample girth with a very fat head, found it most comfortable to twine herself in a spiral around the branch. Lying flat on it was out of the question; she was simply too chubby to find it comfortable. Mrs. P., however, was suspended from the branch in an artistic configuration halfway between a question mark and an exclamation point. This peculiar geometry was perhaps a reflection of her mental state. *What is happening here?* These four words were spiraling through the length of Mrs. P.'s cylindrical body, and she thought they should be likewise screaming in every mind, gizzard, or whatever of every owl in the tree. Unfortunately, such was not the case.

"Why aren't you down there weaving your way through the harp?" Octavia inquired of Mrs. P.

"Don't be ridiculous. You wouldn't catch me jumping octaves or making music for this stupid ceremony. What do they call themselves — Guardians of the Guardians? All this folderol about guarding the ember! Silly rituals and all."

Octavia gave a funny little pneumatic snort in response to Mrs. P.'s outburst. This was her way of laughing. Mrs. Plithiver was a member of the harp guild directed by Madame Plonk. For centuries, the harp guild had been considered the most prestigious of all the nest-maid snake guilds of the great tree. Half the snakes played the lower strings and half played the upper ones. But there were a precious few, the most talented of the snakes, who were confined to neither. These snakes were called sliptweens, and their job was to jump octaves, which contained all eight tones of the scale. It was an energetic leap they had to make. It took skill, muscle, and timing. In her thinner days Octavia had been a sliptween. However, she had all but retired from the harp. Mrs. P. was now considered one of the finest sliptweens in the history of the tree.

"So how did you get out of playing the harp for this whatever-they-call-it ceremony?"

"I told them I sprung a tendon on that cantata the other night."

"I'm surprised that Otulissa didn't think up some way to excuse herself," Octavia said.

"She should have. I can feel her rage all the way up here."

"I know," Octavia replied.

The two snakes became very still and shut their slitted eyes. From at least forty feet above the Great Hollow, they could feel the waves of anger, frustration, of sheer embarrassment that rose from the Spotted Owl's plumage like thermal drafts on a hot summer day. Such were the sensibilities of a nest-maid snake.

Rough air, to put it mildly, Mrs. P. thought.

On the balcony of the Great Hollow, Otulissa perched, blinking in disbelief. Her gizzard was in a nauseating, dizzying turmoil. Her heart was aggrieved as she watched the tawdry spectacle below. An "Honor Guard"— the term itself made her almost yarp — was flying around the ember, which had been removed from Coryn's hollow and put in the center of the Great Hollow. The old box was encased now in a newer, larger, fancier one that had been designed by Gemma and reluctantly forged by Bubo. It was the Whiskered Screech, Gemma, and the Great Gray, Elyan, who were at the front of the procession of owls that flew in circles around the elaborately "en-hollowed" ember. "En-hollowed"— yet another newly coined term that nearly made a pellet swim up Otulissa's gullet. She swallowed hard and tried not to belch. But perhaps the most revolting word of all right now was "ele-vation." For this was the Elevation ceremony of Gemma, Elyan, and a Barn Owl called Yeena. They were to be ele-vated to the highest of the high honor guards, an order called the Guardians of Guardians, not of the great tree, but of the Ember of Hoole. Madame Plonk's voice soared in a newly composed celebratory song called "Chant of the Ember."

> *Oh, dearest Ember of great Hoole,*
> *guard our tree most great.*
> *Warm our gizzards, make us wise,*
> *lead us in your holy ways.*
> *Give us comfort, let tumult cease,*
> *bless each owl so safe we'll keep.*
> *We sing to you, your glowing splendor*

Radiant with magen's grace.
So we ask that peace be with us,
and in you our trust do place.

Madame Plonk was in full voice. The song was quite beautiful, except for the words, Otulissa thought. And what a bunch of racdrops they were! Look at Madame Plonk, strutting about in the air. One would have thought her a peacock. Yet it wasn't even her own feathers she was showing off. It was the frinking cloak she'd gotten from Trader Mags. It was purple — royal purple as she liked to remind everyone — and it was trimmed in ermine. "Ermine is to eat, not to wear," Otulissa muttered. Another owl, a Barred, swung her head around and blinked furiously at her.

"What did you say?" the owl called Quinta hissed.

"I said" — Otulissa said furiously — "Strumina Von Fleet would stare."

"Huh? I thought you said something about eating ermine."

"No, not at all," Otulissa lied. "Strumina Von Fleet, you might not know her. An ancient sage from the Northern Kingdoms, known as much for her unparalleled elegance as for her brilliant mind. A relative of mine, actually. Thirteenth cousin once removed."

"Sssh!" someone else hissed. "It's almost time for the Ultimate Elevation."

Ultimate Elevation, my butt feathers! Otulissa thought, but she did not say a word this time. One could not be too careful these days.

Something strange had befallen the tree. It had really begun before the Band left but she had not taken notice of it then. The tree seemed to have entered a phase of eternal golden glory. But no one at that time had likened it to the glow of the ember itself. If anything, they spoke of it as a lingering tinge of color from the summer. But now owls compared it to the glow of the ember. It was, they said, as if the radiance of the ember had infused the very fabric of the tree. New nest-maid guilds had been started. One was a choir, the Choir of the Ember, that sang only songs composed for praise of the ember. Another group of nest-maids combined with a smaller group of owls wrote these hymns of praise. Owls who had once spent their days practicing their fighting skills with battle claws and ice swords were now painting and composing poetry. And young'uns were learning at astonishingly accelerated rates. Hatchlings rescued from forest fires were learning how to read almost before their flight feathers had fledged. Fritha, a Pygmy Owl, was well into a study of higher magnetics, reading texts that had stumped Otulissa when she was much older.

All this should have warmed Otulissa's gizzard. But she had felt a creeping dread. Because along with all this knowledge too many of the owls of the tree seemed to be growing more and more obsessed with the ember. The knowledge was not illuminating but seemed shadowed in a strange way — shadowed by the glow of the ember, if such a thing could be. This in itself was somewhat of a puzzle, a conundrum for Otulissa. For like all owls she valued the dark, the shadows. Darkness, the night, shades, and shadows had always been illuminating for owls. They did not fear the times when the moon dwenked to nothingness. They reveled in the long winter nights when the days shortened to mere hours. But now she was begining to think of shadows as dangerous things. She herself had begun to read deeply into philosophical texts about the meaning of light and the absence of light, of darkness in the world of owls.

From her perch in the hollow, she glanced about and caught sight of Eglantine peering with an intensely worried look at her best friend, Primrose, who had been asked for this ceremony to fly with a thimbleful of ashes shed by the ember. The little Pygmy Owl was doing a very good job of it as she turned and banked in a tight circle around the "en-hollowed" ember, casting its ashes in what Otulissa had heard was called the "flight path of Elevation." She had no idea what that meant. Every day there seemed to be a new ritual to be named, to be enacted, to be followed in service to the Ember of Hoole. *What does it all mean?* Otulissa thought. *Why have shadows become dangerous? Why is the world of owls being turned inside out?* She remembered how Soren and Gylfie had told her about the horrors of St. Aggie's, where owls were forced to sleep during the night and work during the day. St. Aggie's had been an inside-out world. Was that what was happening here at the tree? Her gizzard lurched fiercely.

Otulissa suddenly decided that this kind of contemplation and theorizing was impractical. She needed to think back and try to pinpoint when the changes had started. Even before the Band left she realized now that many of the owls had become very concerned about the well-being of the ember. Then, within nights of their leaving, Gemma had introduced the idea of moving the ember to a "safer" place where the watch that Coryn had appointed could better guard it. This suggestion did not seem all that unreasonable at the time. Coryn's hollow was small. Only so many owls could keep an eye on it. It was Elyan who had come up with the notion, despite

Coryn's orders that any guard should be representative of all the creatures of the tree, that, within the watch, there must be an "inner guard," an honor guard. Otulissa, Bubo, Eglantine, and Ruby had voted against this. Fleemus had abstained. But still the measure passed. Then all of a sudden they decided an honor guard wasn't good enough. There had to be an even higher level that had certain military powers, but not an army exactly: a militia that they called the Guardians of the Guardians of the Ember, or the GGE. The creation of the GGE had not been voted upon by parliament. It had just happened. No one was sure how, and now there was this Elevation! Elyan, Gemma, and Yeena, members of the militia through some complicated procedure, had been "Elevated." Otulissa, in reviewing the course of events, realized it had begun to accelerate with a visit from Trader Mags.

The magpie trader had discovered some new ruins of the Others and had arrived with a load of her cheap and tawdry gewgaws, including funny-looking hats that no owl could actually wear. One of these had become the "sacred ash bin" for the cold ashes scraped from the ember's container. Mags also had brought scraps of ermine that Madame Plonk immediately claimed. "Ceremonial, dear! Them's the robes of state," Mags kept saying. "Yes, I really lucked out this time. One of them queens or kings of the

Others had kept a stash in this place." Souvenirs from coronations, from rituals of the Others' churches, piles of cloth stitched with silver and gilt thread provided enough to start yet another guild among the nest-maid snakes, a fine embroidery and sewing guild. Mags had hired a dozen helpers to transport all the loot. She had helpfully brought along some pictures of a queen and her attendants as well as many of the Others' church leaders all dressed up for celebrations of their own Glaux, so that the owls of the tree could see the costume and pomp of the Others.

Oh, how Otulissa rued the day Mags had arrived with all this junk! What would that sweet-faced queen with her kind blue eyes have thought of a bunch of owls flapping through the air wearing all her royal trappings? *We're owls, for Glaux's sake, not Others!* Again Otulissa clamped her beak shut for fear the words might escape.

The procession was quite a spectacle. She saw a small company of Northern Saw-whets and Pygmy swoop down from above. On their heads the owls wore ivory thimbles, like the one that Primrose had flown with. They deposited the thimbles in a row near the ember. Some ashes were poured into the thimbles. Near them was a set of decorated teacups and some more ashes were placed in these. Analysis of the ember's sparks and ashes had become a favorite field of study for many owls, especially among the

GGE. A ritual had even been invented that involved the dusting of ashes on the wing tips of those owls about to be Elevated to the position of High Owls of the Ember. It was all just too ridiculous to even imagine owls doing. But the problem was someone had imagined it. And not just one owl, but several. Were they so bored in these times of peace and prosperity that their minds had turned to this senseless veneration, this worship of a coal? Of course Otulissa knew that it was no mere coal. Indeed, it was an ember that possessed great powers that could be used for good or for evil. That was the lesson of the legends. And it was true that one must be vigilant not to let a graymalkin get close, an owl like Nyra, to be precise. But nowhere did legends suggest anything more than vigilance. How had all this *veneration* come about? And so quickly? The Band and Coryn had barely been gone a moon cycle. How she wished they would come back soon. Then perhaps all this would end. But would it? Otulissa felt her gizzard tremble.

CHAPTER NINE

Coryn Sneaks Out

Luckily for Coryn, the hollow where he and the Band had settled was not that far from the Shadow Forest. And the winds had eased up. So he hoped he could make quick work of this. He would go back to the region near the pond where he had spent the better part of a winter after escaping from Nyra and the Pure Ones. It was there that he had first encountered the rabbit. As he flew in the broad light of day, he kept a sharp lookout for crows but so far had seen none. And as he approached the old fallen tree trunk where he had lived, he felt a flutter in his gizzard. Would the rabbit still be there? It seemed almost impossible that a rabbit in these woods thick with owls could have survived so long — even a mystic one. The scene was still so vivid in Coryn's mind. He had seen the plump, succulent rabbit, sitting perfectly still, as if transfixed, in front of a beautiful spiderweb. The rabbit was studying the designs in the web, "reading" them, he said. Their conversation came back to Coryn now.

"I'm a mystic of sorts," the rabbit had begun to explain when Coryn asked him what he was doing. "I see certain things where others don't."

"In a spiderweb?"

"Precisely. I'm a web reader."

But right now as Coryn flew across the pond, the rabbit was nowhere in sight. Coryn spent several hours scouring the surrounding region. He knew time was running out. To fly back to the hollow in the fir tree in Silverveil he would now have to fly against the rising wind. The Band would be worried, possibly furious. The sun was sinking fast. He knew he could not spend any more time. He made one more circle around the pond. Still no sign of the rabbit. So he climbed high above the forest, turned toward Silverveil, and flew on.

He had not been flying long when he picked up a raucous din on the edges of the wind. *By Glaux, that sounds like a grog tree.* Soren had told him that grog trees had begun to reappear in the Southern Kingdoms shortly after the Battle of the Burning in the canyonlands. He had never been to one and he thought this might just be the time. What better place to pick up gossip? But would he be recognized? Most assuredly so. The scar that slashed across his face was a mirror image of Nyra's. They knew that he was not Nyra, but they also knew that he was a king and the inheritor of the ember. *Gadfeathers!* The word exploded in his brain and sent his gizzard into a tizzy. Hadn't Soren also said that gadfeathers were returning? Maybe he could disguise himself!

Gadfeathers, known for their singing as well as their garish ways, festooned themselves with all manner of discarded feathers from other birds, twigs, strands of ivy — whatever was available. *But what if they ask me to sing?* Coryn blinked. He had no idea if he could sing. He wasn't a Snowy or a Boreal Owl, who were known for their fine voices. He supposed he could try. The whole idea was a bit overwhelming. Then a strange quiver moved through his gizzard as he remembered that in the last of the legends, King Hoole had gone in gadfeather disguise.

He alighted in an oak tree overgrown with lovely ever-ivy, a variety that stayed green year round. He could drape some over his head to disguise the scar. There were even some scarlet winter berries growing on a vine as well. But could he sing? He shut his eyes tight and tried to remember one of the old songs from the legends that the Snow Rose, a very famous gadfeather, had sung. It was about wandering and freedom and might appeal to the crowd at a grog tree. He tried a few lines of the song.

I'll find a feather for your ruff,
fly away with me till dawn.

Fly away then we'll be gone.
Hollows we shall leave behind,
fly to places they'll never find.

For a Barn Owl, he didn't sound all that bad. Granted, he was no Madame Plonk — but he wasn't a total disaster either. *Well, here goes,* he thought as he tore off a length of ivy and draped it across his face and tucked bright red winter berry twiglets into his tail feathers. He launched himself off the oak branch, feeling ridiculous but resolved, and headed toward the grog tree. The north side of the tree, a sycamore with dozens of low-spreading limbs, was vacant. All the owls had congregated in the lower branches on the south side of the tree. He soon saw why. Sparkling in the setting sun were the bright and gaudy wares of none other than Trader Mags. She had spread her goods on a deep purple velvet cloak. "Oh, yes, dearie," he heard her saying, "this here represents my new discovery. Bubbles, go fetch them ermine trimmings like I sold Madame Plonk."

"Oh, Madame Plonk bought some of these?" Coryn heard an owl ask. Madame Plonk was known throughout the owl kingdom not only for her magnificent voice but for her glamour.

"Yes, darlin', and this purple cloth with the tufts of ermine would look fabulous on you."

"She's getting on — ain't she now? I'm surprised she can haul this stuff around on her back while she sings."

"She ain't as young as you, darlin'." Trader Mags was loathe to bad-beak her most devoted client. "She mostly wears it in her apartment for high tea. Speaking of which, some time ago I sold her my last coronation teacup. But I might have a line on where I can get another."

Coryn hid in the shadows of the tree. He had a perfect view of the goods and it was not the "gewgaws," as Otulissa called Trader Mags's glittery wares, that attracted him but a tattered old book off to one side. The cover was made from lemming skins. There was only one place where lemmings lived and that was in the Northern Kingdoms, or the N'yrthghar, as it had once been called. On the front of the book an odd design had been etched. Coryn's gizzard grew still and then twisted violently. It was the image of a strange bird — a cross between an owl and a puffin. A puffowl! The result of a monstrous experiment — the creation of that supreme hagsfiend — Kreeth. That was her book! *The Book of Kreeth!*

CHAPTER TEN

The Nature of Hagsfiends Is Discussed

Look, I know you are all angry with me for sneaking off," Coryn turned his head and looked slyly at the Band, "but it isn't as if I invented sneaking off. Didn't I spend my first day of this expedition listening to stories about the four of you sneaking off from the great tree?"

"Point well made," Soren conceded.

"But why? Why did you do this and leave us all worried to death?" Gylfie pressed. "You're not just any owl, Coryn. You are the king."

"Yes, exactly. I am not just any owl." He hesitated. "But it had nothing to do with my being king."

Soren suddenly wilfed and felt an alarming tremor in his gizzard. *He's not going to tell them . . . is he?* At that moment Coryn seemed to almost read Soren's mind and spun his head toward his uncle. "They have to know, Soren. It's time."

"Have to know what? Time for what?" Digger asked. Digger, Twilight, and Gylfie nervously exchanged glances.

Soren closed his eyes and tried to still his gizzard. Perhaps Coryn was right. Perhaps they did have to know, and maybe bringing it out in the open would lessen Coryn's obsession with his mother.

"I think my mother, Nyra, is a hagsfiend."

Digger, Twilight, and Gylfie wilfed. Even burly Twilight was a mere misty shadow of his former self. "That can't be true," he whispered hoarsely.

Soren stepped forward. He had to say something.

"Don't deny it, Soren!" Coryn said. There was a sharpness in his voice that the others had never heard before.

"It's not a question of denying. We have no proof — only suspicions. It is more complicated than Coryn suggests," Soren spoke softly.

"I am sure it is," Digger said. Digger was the most philosophical of the Band. He did not accept the surface meaning of things but, as his name suggested, seemed compelled to dig deeper to find an unexpected truth.

"If Nyra's a hagsfiend, then you ... well, look, you either are or you aren't!" snapped Twilight. Then suddenly the Great Gray was taken aback by his own words. "I mean, it's not like we don't like you."

"Oh, shut up, Twilight!" Digger barked in a most unphilosophical tone of voice.

"I'm only saying it's action not words that count. And Coryn doesn't act haggish."

Digger blinked. "Why, Twilight. That's an astounding insight. I couldn't have said it better myself."

"Well, then quit telling me to shut up. I said it in half the words you would have used, Digger."

"But is there more, Coryn?" Digger added.

"Tell them," Soren said in a quiet voice that he hoped belied his desperation.

"The nature of hagsfiends as we know them has changed over hundreds and thousands of years. Most of us in this modern age have had an encounter with one, but they are powerless wisps that appear but rarely, usually when we are flying and are extremely tired. They are the crows of the night, which makes some kind of sense, since it was originally proposed that they were some sort of mistake of natural history appearing millions of years ago when birds first separated into different species — a mishmash of things that never quite sorted itself out. In the ancient times of nachtmagen, they were quite dangerous."

Soren coughed. "If I might interrupt. That is precisely my point. This is a different era. There is no evidence that

Nyra is anything more than a bad, evil owl. My own brother, your father, Kludd, was a bad, evil owl."

"But my mother's face is monstrously large, unusually large for a Barn Owl, and so is mine."

"It is not faces, not color, not appearances that matter. That was the essence of the Pure Ones' stupidity. They believed that Barn Owls were a superior species of owls. Such reasoning discounted everything else," Soren said fiercely.

Coryn now blinked his eyes tightly shut for several seconds. "All right. I will agree with you that there is no evidence. And until now, or at least very recently, I was wrongly obsessed with my identity. Had I inherited this terrible legacy? It haunted me constantly. I realize now that was wrong of me. It was self-indulgent and inappropriate for a leader, let alone a king. But there is something else that I discovered when I sneaked off."

Soren's gizzard had just started to settle down, but a new turmoil now roiled within in it. "What is it?" he said. Dread seemed to tremble on the edge of those three simple words.

"There is a book. It is in the possession of Trader Mags."

"Yes, and what is the book?" Gylfie said slowly.

"On its cover is a design."

"A design of what, for Glaux's sake?" Twilight fumed.

"A puffowl."

The four members of the Band were suddenly struck dumb.

"Listen to me carefully, now," Coryn said.

Soren blinked and looked at his nephew. *This is a king speaking. Not a self-absorbed young owl having an identity crisis.*

"We know from reading the legends that Kreeth died in that last battle, in the battle for the Ice Palace. Duncan MacDuncan, the wolf, killed her. We know that she never mated. Never had offspring. Therefore her line of hags-fiends died out. But we all know that ideas, good or evil, have longer lives than we mere mortals. It is proven by our libraries, and the libraries at the Palace of Mists. And so this book in which Kreeth wrote her formulas and her fiendish thoughts exists and has existed throughout the centuries." Coryn paused. He saw a mixture of fear and confusion in the four owls' eyes. "I would have tried to bargain for it. But it's a big book. And I didn't have my botkin. There was no way I could have carried it by myself."

"But it's just words," Twilight said defiantly.

"Words, as you well know, can be powerful," Digger replied. "What are you getting at, Coryn?"

"You are right. If Kreeth's words have managed to

survive all these years, even if this book had remained unknown, hidden away, lost, might not some monstrous remnant of her experiments survived in some form or another? And now that the ember has been retrieved we all know that with it comes the possibility for good magic and bad, or nachtmagen. Yes, those hagsfiends that we have all encountered like wisps from a bad dream are impotent. However, they are but one form. Now that the ember is back, there is the possibility that nachtmagen will strengthen these impotent, powerless hagsfiends."

Especially, Soren thought, *if they had the book of the arch hagsfiend, Kreeth.*

"So you are saying that Nyra could be transformed — if indeed she lives." Soren looked hard at his nephew.

"Wasn't she bad enough already?" Twilight asked.

"Maybe," Coryn said, "haggishness is like a disease, which lies dormant for years upon years and when the conditions are right begins to flourish again."

Flourish, thought Soren. He was beginning to despise the word. The great tree now so often called the Golden Tree was said to flourish magnificently. But when Soren thought of those shimmering limbs with their sparkling leaves, he imagined them reaching up to and piercing the ether veil of the owl universe.

Oh, how Soren longed for the days when the Golden Tree was just the great tree. Was that wrong? Was it treasonous to think this way? The world had seemed so dangerous back then. But it was a danger one could see. Pure Ones were Pure Ones. Flecks were flecks. St. Aggie's thugs were . . . well . . . St. Aggie's thugs. You knew who the enemy was. You had an idea of where it might lurk. But this was entirely different. Nyra was not really the enemy. She was merely an agent, the instrument through which an ancient kind of evil, nachtmagen, could be made possible. Nachtmagen itself was the enemy, and how could you fight that?

CHAPTER ELEVEN
The Ether Veil

Soren flew in a luminous golden light. He felt his white face gilded by it, and when he looked down he saw that his white-feathered legs appeared to have been dipped in gold. At that moment he noticed a tiny silver glint like a minuscule fracture in the golden light all about him. He felt his gizzard freeze. His wings grow heavy. *A slit! A tiny slit in the ether veil.* Then he saw another and another. The slits widened, the tips of haggish black feathers began to push through. Suddenly, the golden light bristled with black points. *This is not budging. This is not the same as when our primaries begin to emerge. This is the ether veil shredding!* "Don't wait for me!" a familiar voice screamed. "I am beyond all help! Go! Go! They're back!"

Who? Who is that screaming in my dream? Soren thought. Then, *I am going yeep. Yeep in my own dream. The owl world dies!*

"Soren, wake up! Wake up!" Gylfie was flying up and down in front of his face and batting the air with her tiny wings trying to bring him out of his dream. *How many times have I done this?* she thought. But since he was known to have starsight, Soren and his dreams were not to be ignored. The owls were now all awake. Gylfie turned to them as she continued to fan Soren with her wings. "Bad dream."

"Uh-oh!" Twilight said. He shook his head violently, spinning it this way and that, as if to clear his head of grogginess. "Like we haven't had enough bad news already."

"Just put a mouse in it, Twilight." Gylfie scowled. Then she turned to Soren. "You awake now?"

"Yes." Although as was usually the case he could not remember any details of the dream. "We have to find that book." This was the only thing he could say.

"Where do we start?" Digger asked.

"Find Trader Mags, of course," Coryn said.

"She doesn't like visitors," Gylfie said. "She always thinks they're trying to get a discount."

"Yeah, well, she adds on such a huge transport charge. It's ridiculous," Twilight huffed.

"Is she still in that chapel ruin?" Digger asked.

"I would imagine so," Soren replied. "What time is it now?" he said, peering out of the hollow. The sun flared red through the trees.

"Still a while until tween time and then another half hour till First Black."

Soren peered out. "We'll go at First Lavender."

Owls were keenly aware of every shade in the changing spectrum of a rising and setting sun for each season of the year. Tween time was the last drop of sun before first shadows of twilight, which at this time of year were a frail lavender color. The owls waited impatiently in silence as they watched the sun set.

"All right!" Soren said. "We're off."

Five owls flew out of the fir tree hollow, Soren with Coryn at his side. As soon as they were clear of the tree they rearranged themselves into a tightly packed formation. Twilight flew point, Coryn to starboard, Soren to port, Digger flew tail position, and Gylfie was in the center. Twilight was always the lead owl in conditions of dramatically changing light. He had an extraordinary ability to see in that silvery border between day and night — at twilight when the boundaries became dim and the very shapes of things seemed to melt away.

Coryn could not help but think how different this was from their flight across the Sea of Hoolemere when they had told wet poop jokes, laughed, and even sung. *It's all so different now*, Coryn thought. How horrible to think that the terrible book was in the same world as they were. What was happening? He was king, but how could he fight hagsfiends or whatever monstrosities had slipped through the ether veil? He knew in his gizzard that was what Soren had dreamed of. It must have been a terrible dream. Why, he wondered, had this not happened when Hoole was king? Had he, Coryn, done something wrong? Was it because he was the child of Nyra and Kludd? All these thoughts ran through Coryn's head as they flew on toward the chapel of Trader Mags.

CHAPTER TWELVE
A Visit with Trader Mags

Book? What book? You know I deal with so many arti-
cles. I got me a large inventory these days, Soren,
dearie."

Twilight stepped forward, his plumage bristling so
much that he seemed to swell to half again his normal
size. "Drop the dearies, sweetheart. We know you ain't no
scholar. You don't get that many books running through
this outfit of yours."

"Oh, beggin' your pardon, sir." Bubbles, a smaller magpie, lighted down on the stone floor next to her boss.
"Them books don't run. Don't fly, neither. No, they more
or less flutter. Their pages, that is."

"Shut your frinkin' beak!" Trader Mags' shrill squawk
echoed through the chapel, rousing the last clutch of
snoozing bats from the rafters. Soren felt a slight tremor
pass through his gizzard. Ever since that one bloody night
in St. Aggie's long before his flight feathers had fledged,

the sight of bats had made him feel weak. The owls of St. Aggie's had a savage practice in which they would summon flocks of vampire bats to suck the blood from young owls on the brink of fledging. The bats would take just enough blood to quell the owls' desire to fly. Now Soren, Twilight, and Trader Mags, purveyor of fine goods, stood in a pool of crimson light reflected from the remains of a rose-colored stained-glass window through which the moon shined. The light, the leathery flap of the bats' wings transported him back to that bloody night so long ago. He shook his head. His patience with Mags was wearing thin.

"Look, Mags, enough of this. We know you had the book. It was reported seen at a grog tree."

"By a slipgizzle?" she said in a more timid voice now.

"Precisely," Digger said, walking forward on his long featherless legs. "A slipgizzle of the king's."

"Oh, I see," Trader Mags said primly, and readjusted the jaunty bandanna that covered one eye.

The king perched, unnoticed, in a shadowy corner of the chapel.

"Yes," she said, sighing, "there was a book. Big old thing despite the fact that some of its pages were missing. An old soldier, I think, wanted it. He had to carry it off in a botkin." Coryn felt a twinge in his gizzard. *Soldier? What soldier?*

"What soldier?" Soren said aloud, echoing Coryn's thoughts.

"Well, soldier or hireclaw, not sure. But hireclaw most likely," Mags replied.

"What did he look like?" Twilight asked.

Mags hesitated. Twilight swelled now until he looked like a feathery cloud-streaked moon rolled down from the sky. "C'mon! C'mon! Make it snappy."

Any trace of composure Trader Mags possessed now vanished. Her beak began clacking nervously. "I c-c-can't say. I can't say," she stammered.

"Can't or won't?" Twilight said sharply.

Mags wheeled around to Soren and looked at him beseechingly with her tiny, piercing black eyes. Soren remained impassive. In a flash, Twilight tore off the bandanna. The owls gasped. A bald spot in the magnificent glistening black plumage was revealed. Trader Mags shrieked.

"Cover her up. Give her back the bandanna! For Glaux's sake," Soren ordered.

"Don't be such a thug, Twilight," Gylfie scolded.

"We need some answers here," Twilight shot back.

"Oh, that hireclaw, he was a thug all right," Trader Mags muttered.

"Oh, ma'am, I be so sorry," Bubbles broke in, gushing with sympathy. "Never knew you got the feather blight. And on your head! How unfortunate," she said, picking up the bandanna to give to her boss.

"Better bald than brainless, you twit!" Trader Mags lashed out at the smaller magpie with one wing and swatted her across the floor. She then turned to Soren. "He didn't give a name. I can only tell you that he was an unusually large Barn Owl."

Coryn felt a turbulence mounting in his gizzard. "Any distinguishing characteristics? Marks?" *Don't say it! Don't say it!* he thought.

"Yes, as a matter of fact. A large nick out of his beak."

She had said it. She might as well have shouted his name out loud. *Stryker!* One of Nyra's top lieutenants. Lieutenant Major Stryker of the Pure Ones, and he had received that wound in the Battle of the Burning. Trader Mags, of course, did not know his name or much else about him aside from the nick in his beak.

"I don't know," she said repeatedly to each question as it was asked. "I don't know where he flew in from. . . . No, Gylfie, no idea where he was going."

"Did he talk much?"

"Not really."

"Did he know Krakish?" Digger asked.

"What in hagsmire is Krakish?" Trader Mags asked.

"The language of the Northern Kingdoms," Soren replied.

"I don't know if he knew it," she paused. "But . . ."

"But what?" Twilight pressed.

She looked at him nastily. Then spat the words out. "He didn't have to know much freakish."

"Krakish," Gylfie corrected. "Why not?"

"'Cause there wasn't many words in that book. Mostly pictures. Worst, ugliest pictures you ever seen. To tell the truth, I was glad to get rid of the frinkin' thing."

"Well." Soren sighed, realizing that getting more information was a lost cause. "You've been most helpful, Mags. I'm sorry about the bandanna." She had retied it on her head and looked up beseechingly. "You won't go telling now about me bald spot, will ya, Soren? It'd just tear me up somethin' fierce."

"No, of course not."

"You know, Mags, if you took off that bandanna some of the time and let the air get at it, your feathers might come back," Gylfie offered.

"I'm attached to it," she said without a trace of sentiment in her voice, and looked furiously at Twilight with her beady black eyes. Then she turned to the others. "Are you sure I can't interest you in something? You know, I found this new site. And I got me some lovely porcelain things back in the sacristy. Bubbles, go fetch them demitasse cups."

Soren felt obliged to at least look at the wares after having caused her so much trouble and embarrassment. Maybe he could bring back a present for the three Bs, as his chicks were sometimes called. They were always wanting presents when he came back from hunting. It seemed like just bringing in a vole was not quite sufficient these days. Bubbles arrived with a botkin, and Mags drew from it several little cups.

"They ain't teacups exactly. They calls them demitasses. At least, so Madame Plonk tells me. Now, mind you, they ain't as big and as fancy as that lovely coronation teacup of Madame Plonk's. But they be awfully pretty. So dainty, ain't they?"

Soren could imagine Basha, Blythe, and Bell eating dried caterpillars out of them. "What'll you take for them?" he asked.

"Oh, let's see. I've had a hankering for some yoick

stones." Yoick stones were small rocks with traces of both gold and silver that could be smashed by a Rogue smith and then fired to release the silver and gold, even though it was an inferior grade of these two metals.

"Don't have any," Soren said. "How about a fine rabbit skin?"

"Perhaps."

"Digger, will you get the botkin with the skin?"

Digger went out, returning quickly, and spread the skin on the stone floor.

"Killed him myself," Twilight said.

"I don't doubt it," Mags said as she carefully stepped around the skin, examining it.

"It was an artistic kill if I do say so." Twilight's voice brimmed with pride.

Trader Mags stopped in her tracks. "There ain't no such thing, you brute, as an artistic kill!" She then looked up at Soren. "I'll take it."

So the deal was made and the owls were off. The night was still long. "I'd say," Digger began, "that you, Twilight, are not high on Trader Mags' list of favorite creatures."

"That's the least of our problems," Gylfie said. "Where in the world are we going to find this owl with the book? We don't even know his name."

"His name is Stryker and he was my mother's top lieutenant."

"Our worst fear," Gylfie moaned.

"Not exactly," Coryn said cryptically. The other four owls spun their heads to look at Coryn. "Our worst fear is a half-made hagsfiend with a book on how to finish the job."

"But the book," Digger said. "What little we know from reading the legends did not tell how to make a hagsfiend but how to create new monsters. Hagsfiends were born, not made."

Now all the owls peered at Digger. "That is small comfort, Digger!" Gylfie said. "A monster? A hagsfiend? Not exactly delightful company."

"Words, just words," muttered Twilight.

"Quit squabbling!" Coryn barked. He was trying to think how they might find Stryker. Where he might be. For a long time, the Pure Ones had been encamped in the canyonlands. But they had been routed by war and must have moved by now. If he could get some coals from a Rogue smith's forge they could kindle a fire. Just a small one that might yield a few hints as to where the old lieutenant might be. But Coryn knew from past experience that his firesight never seemed to work very well when he sought specific answers. The images were often vague and confusing. The flames did not like to be forced. They yielded what they would at their own whim and not on demand. As he was thinking about this, he caught a glimpse of something sparkling beneath them. Like diamonds strung through winter grass, a spiderweb hung in the night. And then a rapid heartbeat. *The rabbit!*

CHAPTER THIRTEEN

The Coronation Teacup

Otulissa had been busy in the library for at least half the day and had not yet slept. As she flew back to her hollow through the strands of golden milkberry vines and heard the soft susurrus of stirring leaves, she thought how wrong all this felt. *It's the time of the white rain, for Glaux's sake. It's winter. Winter everyplace but here*, she thought miserably. The golden strands should be withered and white. The berries should be shriveled and even whiter and there should be no leaves. The tree should loom dark, stripped of the splendors of summer or autumn. That was the way it was supposed to be. Was she the only owl feeling this way, she wondered. She was pretty sure that Soren's mate was not all that pleased with this perpetual summer. But of course, Pelli was so busy with her three owlets she barely had time to worry. *Fine thing, Soren going off like that just when the Bs were about to learn how to fly! Males!* She'd never mate. *Well*, she thought, *one should never say never.* She felt a little squeeze in her gizzard as she thought

93

of Cleve. A gizzard squeeze was the closest an owl came to blushing.

Cleve was a dear friend whom she had met in the Northern Kingdoms. He lived at the Glauxian retreat on the island in the Bitter Sea. He was a healer and was continuing his study of medicine. So far he had not taken vows. *I'll smack him if he does!* Otulissa thought. *Cancel that! What a terrible thing to even think of dear Cleve.* But she knew that if they mated, there would be a mess of hatchlings, and guess who would get stuck taking care of them? Otulissa wasn't really mother material. She loved young-'uns. But how could she raise chicks in a proper manner, head up the Ga'Hoology chaw, fly weather and colliering, teach the history of the tree, and give special seminars in higher magnetics, all on her own? She was one of the busiest rybs in the entire tree. No, it was out of the question.

But then she returned to her original question: Was she the only one disturbed by the unchanging nature of the tree, this so-called Golden Tree that seemed condemned to a perpetual summer, that shed very few of its leaves? And those leaves that did drop left behind odd golden traceries like some sort of scroom. *A scroom tree?* she wondered. Taking one more look at the branches of the tree before she entered her own hollow, she thought for perhaps the thousandth time how peculiar everything felt.

She was fairly sure that Eglantine didn't think things were normal. And Eglantine had hemmed and hawed and not yet given an answer about participating in one of the endless rituals that the GGE was always dreaming up. But Primrose, Eglantine's best friend, seemed most enthralled with all the ceremonies and had agreed to become an acolyte at the altar of the ashes that were collected from the ember.

Otulissa alighted on the branch outside her hollow. There was a cross fire of brilliance that almost hurt her eyes as the midday sun reflected off the golden vines and limbs of the tree. Years before they would have called this a perfect late-summer day — the milkberries approaching the copper rose color of early fall would indeed have a special luminosity on a day like this. Owls would even get up from their daytime sleep for a glimpse of such splendor. But now it did not seem splendid. Too much of a good thing and, alas, even beauty becomes quite ordinary. *Even vulgar. Yes, vulgar. The tree is vulgar.* Otulissa sniffed. "Vulgar" was one of her favorite words. Tawdry, vulgar, coarse, gaudy, ostentatious, flashy — like Madame Plonk. Madame Plonk was all of those words.

"Oh, great Glaux, Madame Plonk! You scared the living nightlights out of me!" Otulissa gasped as the Great Snowy entered her hollow. Indeed, none other than Madame

Plonk perched just inside Otulissa's hollow. She looked in all her frippery about as out of place among Otulissa's simple furnishings — books, maps, and such — as golden milkberries in winter.

"I know we've had our differences but . . ." Madame Plonk began.

"We *are* different." Otulissa blinked. There was no owl who could be more different from herself than Madame Plonk. Right now, however, Otulissa had to admit she had never seen Madame Plonk look so sad — indeed, devastated. "Whatever is the problem, Madame Plonk?" And she was tempted to add, *How could I ever help you with any problem you might have?*

"It's my teacup." Madame Plonk's eyes welled up with tears.

"Your teacup?" Otulissa was bewildered. *What in Glaux's name is she talking about?* And the way she was scratching her breast with one talon suggested that her teacup was some vital organ that had begun to act up. "Madame Plonk, I am not quite following you. Your teacup?"

"My coronation teacup. I've had it for years." She sobbed and collapsed now from the guest perch into a small mountain of white feathers.

"Pull yourself together, Madame Plonk. This is most unseemly. Get a grip!"

The Snowy picked up her large head. "You don't remember? You helped me read the numbers and the name. I'm not as smart as you and you were so kind."

Aahh, the pellet drops! Otulissa thought, but did not say so out loud. It was a crude expression for finally remembering something. She did remember the teacup now. It was another gewgaw that Plonk had gotten from Trader Mags. Yes, there was a picture of a female Other wearing a crown gazing out with great dignity, a dignity that far exceeded anything Madame Plonk could ever aspire to. And there were numbers. "One-nine-five-three. Yes, of course."

"Queen E, you remember?"

"Yes, I can't imagine why anyone would give a one-letter name to a queen. One must assume the rest of the letters were worn away though time. So what is the problem?"

The very question threw Madame Plonk into a new fit of sobs. She was beating her wings now on the floor of the hollow. To Otulissa, she seemed like an actress who was enjoying her own performance a bit too much. But then again, there was something rather gizzard-rending when she began to speak. "You cannot imagine how, over all these years as the dark fades from the day, after I have sung 'Night Is Done' and all the owls go to rest, how wonderful it is to settle on the branch just outside my hollow with my coronation cup filled with milkberry tea. So restorative to not only the voice but the spirits. I watch the sun creep up over the horizon."

Great Glaux, she's waxing absolutely poetic! Otulissa thought as Madame Plonk wiped away a tear.

"And now would you believe it?"

"Believe what, Madame Plonk?" Otulissa said gently.

"They want, no, they demand, my coronation teacup."

She flopped down again with a huge sob. *Great Glaux in glaumora, what am I going to do with this . . . this . . . thing?* Otulissa thought as she regarded the heaving heap of white fluff. She sighed deeply and then spoke calmly. "Who precisely wants the teacup?"

Madame Plonk raised her head and said crossly, "Not just any teacup, the coronation teacup of Queen E."

"All right, who wants the coronation teacup of Queen E, and why?"

"The acolytes of the altar."

"Oh, racdrops!" Otulissa exploded. "Whatever for?"

"The sacred ashes of the ember."

"Oh, now they've really gone too far," Otulissa said. And apparently they truly had, for Madame Plonk, who had enjoyed until now all the ridiculous vulgar ritual of what was being called the "cult of the ember," was fed up.

Otulissa spoke briskly. "I don't know when this

stupidity will end, but surely Primrose could help you out. She's an acolyte, isn't she?"

"She is, but she is . . . I don't know how to put it. . . . She is really enjoying being one. She's changed. Even Eglantine says so. And you know she's writing plays now."

"Yes, I heard that. I heard that she's quite good."

"Yes, odd, isn't it? All of us in some way have been able to do so much more. Why, I never thought that I could ever reach those high notes in the moonlight cantata with hardly taking a breath but since the ember arrived I can." She paused and raised her head. Her yellow eyes turned hard. "BUT I DON'T WANT TO DO THIS! I WON'T GIVE UP MY CORONATION TEACUP."

"But what can I do about it, Madame Plonk?"

"Hide it, please, Otulissa. No one would ever suspect that such a rare and beautiful thing would be kept here." She looked about the spare hollow not so much with disdain as pity.

Otulissa would never know quite what made her agree to take the teacup, but she did. Perhaps it was just the wrongness of the tree and the stupidity of all this ritual. What, indeed, gave these idiot owls the right to commandeer personal possessions for their ridiculous rituals? Acolytes of the ashes! And that Primrose, a very sensible owl, a responsible member of the search-and-rescue chaw, had bought into it! *Well, I shall have a very serious talk with her,* Otulissa thought. But then she thought again. She knew she wouldn't. Teacups might be hidden, but words could be overheard, could leak out, and she had noticed that for the first time in all the years she had been at the Great Ga'Hoole Tree, the owls in this golden era had become more guarded. They were frightened to say what they really thought. Indeed, what was considered a great flourishing of the Golden Tree could be the beginning of its death. How she longed for a true season of white rain, when the berries would turn the color of dried bones and the tree, leafless, would look grim and dignified with its dark limbs spreading like a black skeleton against a wintry sky.

CHAPTER FOURTEEN
The Rabbit at Last

Coryn motioned to the Band to hold back and remain on the limb where they had just lighted down while he settled silently on the ground near the rabbit. In a pool of moonlight, it stood seemingly frozen in front of a spiderweb. As rabbits went, this was not an especially impressive one. Small of stature, with an undistinguished brownish-gray pelt, it was completely unremarkable except for the white crescent on its forehead. This, in fact, was the signifying mark of a web reader, a mystic rabbit who could read in the webs of spiders "tidings," as the rabbit called them, from the present, the future, and the past. But the information was most often incomplete and vague. It came in fragments, the rabbit had explained to Coryn, much like the pieces of a puzzle.

There was no greeting, and the rabbit did not deflect its gaze from the web. It merely took up as if there had been no interruption between that first time it had met

101

Coryn and now. "A dark feather, ashes, bone. Is it now? Was it then? Or is it yet to come?"

Coryn knew better than to ask a specific question. If he did, the rabbit would give him a very confusing answer. But he could not help it. "Is it something about me?"

The rabbit finally turned slowly toward him. "Me . . . me . . . me. Aaah, youth! Even with kings, it's all about me, me, me."

The four other owls fluttered down and stood in a circle around the rabbit. "I wish I could help you more. You're looking for her, aren't you?" Nyra's name did not need to be mentioned. All five owls nodded. "And I can only come up with these three things — a dark feather, ashes, and bone. Coryn has explained to you that I can only offer pieces. I cannot put the puzzle together. And these pieces are very difficult. I am not sure if they are real or just . . . confusing!" the rabbit exclaimed. "What I see in the web is either a wisp or a whisper."

"You can *see* a whisper?" asked Twilight.

"Shhh," said Digger. "You're being too literal."

"If it's a wisp, it is just an escaped thread from a dream. But if it is a whisper, well, it might be real. What I am seeing has the — how should I put it? — the cloudiness of a dream, but there is also an echo."

"Do whispers have echoes?" Twilight asked.

"I asked myself the same question. One does not think of whispers as having echoes. Does one?" The five owls shook their heads. "Unless that is a whisper in a cave."

It was as if a bolt of lightning had shot through Coryn's gizzard. "Bones! Feather! Ashes! Cave! She's in a cave!"

"There are a lot of caves, Coryn," Gylfie said softly.

"No, not just any cave. *The* cave."

The four other owls exchanged skeptical glances.

"The cave of my father's Final ceremony in the canyonlands. She wants his bones, or rather the ashes of his burned bones!"

"Great Glaux!" Digger blurted. "Ashes from a Final ceremony. Kreeth lusted for them. They were a most powerful ingredient for her monstrous experiments."

Twilight had grown very still. He looked toward Coryn. The moonlight glanced off his head, turning his gray feathers silvery. "The cave," he said quietly, "the cave where I killed Kludd in the Battle of the Burning, is that where they had the Marking?" The Final ceremony for a fallen leader was called the Marking.

Coryn nodded. "They had guarded his body day and night so scavengers wouldn't get it and then when there were only bones, they burned them."

"That is odd," Soren said. "For a Final ceremony most owls burn the entire body. Why wait for the bones?"

Coryn opened his eyes wide at his uncle's question and then blinked. Blinked not in surprise but with a strange knowingness. Soren felt a quiver pass through his gizzard. "As I told you before we left, Soren, my mother had a fondness for peculiar rituals, rituals of violence and blood that have roots in a haggish legacy. We know from the legends the power of ashes from bones."

"But she hadn't read the legends," Gylfie said. There was a note of quiet despair in her voice.

"She didn't need to. She *felt* them," Coryn replied evenly.

"So," the rabbit said, turning to the spiderweb again, "it is not a wisp, but a whisper."

"It's real." Twilight said. "Let's fly!"

And as the five owls lofted themselves into the winter night, Twilight had but one thought: *I killed him once. If she conjures him up I'll kill him again . . . and Nyra, too!*

In a distant cave in the canyonlands, an owl hunched over a book. The night was almost moonless; only a thin sliver hung in the sky. But it seemed that the rest of that moon had come down to Earth and sought refuge in this cave, for in the darkness a face like a glistening orb appeared suspended, its surface slashed and cratered with battle wounds.

"I haven't given up on the ember, Stryker," she told her lieutenant. "I was hatched on the night of an eclipse, as was my son, Nyroc." *Never, never shall I call him Coryn,* she silently swore. The years had not done Nyra any favors. Once considered a great beauty, a magnificent specimen of a *Tyto alba,* the loveliest of all Barn Owls, at least as far as the Pure Ones were concerned, she had not weathered well. Her dark eyes had lost their luster. The scar that ran diagonally down her face, a wound from long ago, had widened, leaving an ugly red slash. The unique heart shape of a Barn Owl's face was perhaps its most alluring feature. The contours of the heart usually fringed in short tawny golden feathers had darkened on Nyra's face to a deep muddy brown and grown shaggy, blurring the elegance of the heart shape. In several places, her feathers had grown thin, revealing unsightly patches of skin.

She now looked up at Stryker as if expecting a response. "Yes, General Mam, I know that. I was there — well, not when you were hatched — but I remember quite well the eclipse when Nyroc hatched!"

"And do you know the significance of being born on the night of an eclipse?" Stryker, though no mental giant of a bird, was a survivor, and he knew how to play the game to jolly the General Mam. He knew that she was eager to impart some tidbit of profound knowledge. Ever since he had gotten the book for her she had spent long days studying rather than sleeping. "Well, I'll tell you." She sighed happily. Indeed, this was the happiest he had seen Nyra in a long time. Most of the Pure Ones were dead or gone. Some fled to the Northern Kingdoms—they thought they would be safer in those vast ice-shrouded regions of glaciers and endless winter. Some had vanished into the Beyond and still others had hoped simply to start over, and never to hear the words "Pure Ones" again. In all, there were only five of the original Pure Ones left: Nyra, Stryker, Wortmore, Spyke, and Gebbles.

And there was a new recruit. Hardly a young one and not a Barn Owl, but an ancient Whiskered Screech from the Northern Kingdoms — Ifghar. He claimed that he was the brother of the legendary Ezylryb and he arrived with a Kielian snake named Gragg who, if he could be kept off the bingle juice, was fairly intelligent. They were both frightfully old. Ifghar could barely fly. But they knew war. They knew about fighting, and most important, they knew about ice weapons. The Guardians of Ga'Hoole had won the great battle in the canyonlands, the Battle of the Burning, often called the Battle of Fire and Ice because of the ice weapons that came with the reinforcement troops from the Northern Kingdoms. Since then, they had improved their skills with these weapons and sent regular expeditions to harvest new ones. Stryker hoped this Ifghar and his snake would sooner or later prove useful.

"Let me tell you about the significance of an eclipse." Nyra cocked her head and began to speak in an almost professorial manner. "You see, dear Stryker, when an owl hatches on the night of a lunar eclipse an enchantment can be cast on that creature, a charm that gives that creature unusual powers. Hoole, considered by some the first great king, was hatched on such a night, as was I and my son, Nyroc. An eclipse is coming and with this book that you fetched for me, well . . . I think I can accomplish great things."

"Capture the ember?"

"No, you fool, re-create a creature already hatched. Except I shall make him better this time . . . much better. . . ." Her dull eyes began to glisten ever so slightly, as if deep within them a spark that had long lain dormant had been rekindled.

CHAPTER FIFTEEN

The First Prisoner

Otulissa looked through the bars of the hollow. It was all so unbelievable. A prison at the Great Ga'Hoole Tree! And she, Otulissa, was the first prisoner! She gazed out the window at the wintry sky. It was just First Lavender and in the distance she could see three tiny specks and then a larger one. Her breath caught. It was Pelli and her chicks, Basha, Blythe, and Bell. It was their First Flight ceremony. Otulissa could tell by the configurations they were flying. But why would they be doing it before tween time at First Lavender? How odd. It wasn't as if there were a danger of crows out here on the island. Crows rarely flew across the Sea of Hoolemere. They hated salt water, almost as much as the hagsfiends had in the legends. Then it came to her. A new rule had been instituted that all First Flight ceremonies were supposed to be flown around the altar of the ember and the ashes. *How wrong is that — to have one's First Flight indoors, around some stupid altar and not under a starry sky.* Otulissa sighed and worry stirred her gizzard. "Oh, dear! I hope Pelli knows what she's doing. This could be dangerous for her and the chicks," Otulissa murmured to herself.

Elyan and Gemma had pronounced that certain things were considered *glimpox* — or slanderous — a violation of the sacred nature of the ember. This would certainly be considered glimpox. They'd have to build a new jail. There certainly wasn't room in this one. What was truly glimpox was a jail in the great tree. What could be a worse, a more horrendous violation of the nature of this tree than making a hollow into a jail? It was outrageous, unbelievable. And it had all happened because of that foolish coronation teacup she had agreed to hide for Madame Plonk. Otulissa shut her eyes tight, reliving the horrible moments leading up to her arrest.

Gemma had arrived at her hollow. Her rather skimpy ear tufts stuck up as high as she could manage and twitched as if to add some sort of accent of authority to what she was about to say. "It has been reported that you have in your possession an article that was requisitioned for the vigil of the ashes." Otulissa would not even deign to inquire what in hagsmire was the vigil of the ashes. She didn't care.

"Of what article are you speaking?" Otulissa asked politely.

"The coronation teacup of Madame Plonk."

Otulissa immediately decided to own up to having the teacup and silently cursed Madame Plonk. At least she would not be accused of lying. "Yes, right here."

She fetched the teacup from a cubby in her hollow so quickly that Gemma seemed almost surprised. "Take it," she said, shoving it toward the Whiskered Screech. "I have no use for it."

"Then why did you hide it for Madame Plonk?"

"She merely requested that I keep it for her. I had no idea why." *A tiny lie*, she thought. "But you're more than welcome to it."

Gemma had seemed visibly upset. This had obviously been too easy. "But you were hiding it in that cubby."

"I don't have a lot of room in here, as you can see," Otulissa had said, gesturing with a small sweeping arc of one wing. "I put it out of harm's way."

"Aha!" Gemma screeched, and lofted herself directly into the air. "So you consider myself and the rest of the order of the Guardians of the Guardians of the Ember to be 'harm'?"

"I never said such a thing!"

"Yes, you did, just now. I arrest you for un-emberish glimpox activity. Article One, Section B of the Glimpox Statutes for Protection of the Ember."

With that, three other members of the order, who must have been waiting outside on a close branch, stormed into Otulissa's hollow, and the next thing she knew she was in a prison that she didn't even know existed in the great tree.

She ran her talons over the bars and mused that Bubo himself must have made them. *What must he have thought?* At just that moment, as if reading her mind, there was a flare of ruddy red outside the opening and the old blacksmith appeared.

"Otulissa!" he said in a raw, desperate voice. "I thought I was making rods for still another cage for the ember. I swear, Otulissa. I would have never done it had I known." The Great Horned looked an absolute wreck. His yellow eyes flickered madly.

"Bubo, I know you couldn't have known. No need for an apology."

The light of the setting sun flashed off the bars, tingeing them gold. Bubo squinted and blinked. "It's a terrible time, ain't it?" He shook his head wearily. "What with this Golden Tree and all."

"I'm starting to hate gold," Otulissa said.

"I even think Plonkie's getting a bit disgusted with it all."

"As well she should!" Otulissa scowled.

"Look, don't go too hard on her. She feels terrible about the whole thing."

"Yes, but look who's in prison."

"But she's under 'tree arrest,' as they call it."

"Tree arrest! What will they think of next? What does that mean?"

"She can't leave the tree, but they have to have her around to sing all them new chants for them ceremonies." The very words caused a deep twinge in Otulissa's gizzard as she saw the three Bs completing their First Flight ceremony. *What has happened to the real ceremonies that mark growth and the passages in an owl's life? Ceremonies for an ember — racdrops!* "What are we going to do?" Otulissa sighed. "When will Soren and the Band and the king get back? Coryn would have a fit if he saw this nonsense with the ember."

"I'm thinking, Otulissa, we got to get word to them!"

"But we don't even know where they are."

At that moment, a song began to rise in the tree as Madame Plonk's unearthly voice spiraled up into the soft purple of the twilight. It was a new song that had replaced the old one that hailed the coming of First Black. This one hailed the glow of the ember.

> *Eternal ember, strong and glowing,*
> *let your light suffuse our tree.*

Most holy spirit of the fires,
deliver us from fate most dire.

On the word "dire," there was an ear-shattering crack that resounded throughout the tree. A high flutter could be heard as hundreds of owls flew out from their hollows. The golden leaves of the tree shivered and a few even fell off, drifting lazily toward the ground.

And then the word swirled through the tree. A burly Short-eared Owl flew by the bars of her prison. "Matron! Matron! What is it?" Otulissa called out.

Barely turning around, the matron called back. "It's Madame Plonk. Her voice has cracked!"

CHAPTER SIXTEEN

Cracked

Listen to me, Bubo," Madame Plonk spoke in a low, hoarse voice. Each word was like a rough-edged shard grating against the next. "I got her into this. I've got to get her out of it."

"But not you, Plonkie, dear. You know nothing about flying around out there. When was the last time you crossed Hoolemere? You know nothing about tracking. I should go."

"They're not going to let you go for a minute, Bubo. They got you working that forge all hours. And they'd suspect you. They know how close you are to Coryn and to Soren and the Band." Madame Plonk fixed her old friend in a steady gaze. "Look, even when I hid that cup they didn't really want to punish me because they needed my voice. Same way they need your smithing. Tree arrest. That's a laugh. I was planning this before my voice cracked. It hurts to talk so don't make me explain too much. Just listen. I'm the first to admit that I'm a vain old owl. 'The first singer of the tree' was what they used to call a gadfeather. She was a Snowy like me and my line is descended from hers. Her name was Snow Rose. She not only sang, but she was a heroic owl. She helped save the life of Hoole's mother, Siv, then joined Siv's troops in the Battle in the Beyond when Hoole retrieved the ember." Madame Plonk paused. "I didn't know any of this until I took the cup to Otulissa and had, well, I had my last spot of tea in the coronation cup, and she joined me and told me this part of the old stories. The ones they call the legends. But imagine this Snow Rose, a warrior singer! A soldier singer! It's true. All written down it is in them old books of Ezylryb's. I can do it, too, Bubo. I can be a warrior singer. I know I can."

Bubo looked at her with some alarm. Madame Plonk had led a rather comfortable life, indeed one might say cushy, in that tricked-out hollow of hers that was almost frothy with its trimmings of lace, tassels, gewgaws, and baubles. She was Trader Mags' best customer. The various doodads that Mags stripped from the castles, manor houses, churches, and abbeys of the Others found their way into Madame Plonk's hollow. There were plump cushions stuffed with her own discarded feathers covered in velvet from a prince's cloak. "Gemma and Elyan are so worried about me now since my voice cracked because without it they can't have their stupid rituals. They're smothering me with kindness."

"You're not under tree arrest?"

"No. I told them that I had to be entirely alone if my voice was to come back, that it made me too nervous to have all these matrons and owls checking on me all the time. I can get away, Bubo. I can."

"But, Plonkie."

"Bubbie?" She turned her yellow eyes on him, batted them a few times in a sad yet still flirtatious manner, and implored. "You've got to understand. No one will suspect me if I go."

"But how will you find them? No one knows where they might be."

"I'll go to these grog trees I've heard about. A lot of gossip swirls about in grog trees. If my voice is back, I might sing. Singers in olden days were always welcome at grog trees, Otulissa told me." She shut her eyes for a long time. A very long time, and did not open them when she began to speak. "And it will come back, Bubo, it will. As soon as I get away." She opened her eyes now and looked straight into the Great Horned's eyes. "There is something wrong with the tree, Bubo. You know it as well as I do. It ain't right. Everything looks all gold and glorious but something's amiss. It shames me now to think of meself singing away at all those stupid ceremonies for the frinkin' ember."

"Hush, Plonkie. Mind your beak. They got slipgizzles all over. Can hardly breathe without them listening in."

"Oh, Bubo, but all that nonsense — acolytes of the ashes, the ember procession, the sacred this, the blah-blah that — and I was actually enjoying it for a while. I got to wear that scrap of purple velvet tufted with ermine, and I felt so special."

"You *are* special, Plonkie."

"It's my voice that was special and now it's cracked."

There was a fluttering outside the hollow and the shadow of wings passed through the stream of moonlight. Bubo looked around nervously and then leaned in close to the Snowy so that his beak was almost touching her ear slit. "Plonkie, are you *really* set on doing this?"

"I am, Bubo."

CHAPTER SEVENTEEN
The Shape of the Flames

A wing and a whisper, thought Soren. *Is that all we've got? Yes.* That seemed to be what he, the Band, and Coryn were flying on. It was all too vague. He wanted to be able to trust the strange rabbit's mystic web readings, but it just all seemed so . . . so . . . he searched for the word . . . so *wispy*. So insubstantial. And if Nyra was really there in this cave with whatever remnants of the Pure Ones there might be, things needed to be firmer. They had to plan a strategy. What were they to do? Just fly in and seize the book? Even if they were successful in taking the book, would that be the end of their troubles? It wasn't really the book that was the problem. It was, Soren supposed, the ideas in the book. But ideas could be dangerous just the way the ember could be dangerous in the talons of the wrong owl. He supposed they must fly on. Within a split second of having that thought, he knew he was dead wrong. And as if to confirm his next thought he saw the dark tendrils of smoke rising in the distance.

Soren lifted a port wing, giving the signal to land. They had flown fast from Silverveil and were now on the border between The Barrens and Ambala.

"What are we stopping for? I'm not tired," Coryn asked as they settled into one of the rather puny trees in The Barrens. But Gylfie took one look at Soren and realized immediately that something was disturbing him deeply. The spindly branch could barely support the weight of the five owls and bowed toward the ground.

"Brushfire over there half a league away." Digger nodded toward the rolling smudge of smoke on the horizon.

"I know," Soren said. "That's part of the reason we've stopped."

"What's the other part?" Gylfie asked. She fixed her old friend with a knowing look.

"We're rushing into this."

"What do you mean?" Coryn asked. His voice was slightly strained. "That was one of the clearest readings I've ever gotten from the rabbit."

"You've encountered that rabbit all of two times, Coryn," Soren said. "We need more information. I want to dive into that brushfire. Get some coals and build a small fire here."

Coryn looked somberly at his uncle. "You know I can't just simply ask a fire. That's not how it works."

"I know, Coryn, I know. I don't want you to ask anything. I only want you to watch — just watch. There are hot coals in these brushfires. They'll give you good flames."

Gylfie sighed. "Except for you and Coryn, the rest of us won't be much help in harvesting coals. We're hardly colliers. Too bad Otulissa isn't here."

Soren jerked his head up. He felt a sharp ping in his gizzard and blinked at Gylfie. The moment she said the words "too bad Otulissa isn't here" it reminded him of something.

"What's wrong, Soren?" Gylfie asked.

He shook his head as if to dislodge a thought that had become wedged deep in his brain. "When you said 'Otulissa' it reminded me of something." *Another wisp? A wisp of a dream perhaps?*

An hour later, the five owls backed away from a small fire that they had built with the half dozen or so coals that Soren and Coryn had retrieved. Coryn stood the closest to the fire. He felt clumsy, even stupid. The flames looked so ordinary. This wasn't right. He spun his head around finally. "I don't mean to be rude, but the rest of you get out of here. Scram. I can't do it when you're watching me."

"Of course," Soren said. "We'll go hunting."

Once they were gone, Coryn relaxed. He let the heat

of the flames lick his face. He closed his eyes and watched the red shadows dance jigs on the inside of his eyelids, then opened them again. The moon was rising. More than halfway through its newing, it appeared slightly lopsided, as if it were about to tumble off the horizon. When it was full in a few more days, there would be an eclipse according to Gylfie, who knew the ways of the stars and the planets because she was the navigation ryb. Coryn had been hatched on the night of an eclipse. And so had Hoole, the king of the legends, and so had Nyra. He felt a shiver pass through him. How could the world contain such good and such bad?

And what was he? What if the blood of a hagsfiend really did run through his veins? His mind wandered. The flames cast red silhouettes against the moon that trembled now on the darkening horizon. Odd, but he suddenly realized that he had never seen the flames in just this manner — their silhouettes as opposed to looking directly at them. He could not look into them as deeply, but their contours, their shapes had a new clarity. He saw the shape of an owl. A Whiskered Screech, he was certain. He could tell by the small tuft of feathers that hung from his face. He was not especially strong nor a steady flier, and what was that — a nest-maid snake coiled on his back? A wind stirred the fire and the flames leaped suddenly to one side, stretching, nearly galloping across the silver of the moon. His gizzard gave a small jump. Something so familiar in that shape, but just then low clouds brushed across the moon. "Racdrops!" Coryn muttered, and dropped his gaze to the flames in the fire. Could he find it there? It was the second shape, the second silhouette that intrigued him, and not that of the Whiskered Screech. There was something in that shape, and he was sure that it was not an owl this time that tugged at his very gizzard. He felt a longing, a deep and anguished longing — for a place? For a creature? He peered deeply into the flames. *There are so many different colors in a fire no one would believe it,* thought Coryn. *There is never just red or orange.* Coryn had heard that there were no two snowflakes exactly alike, and he believed that no two flames were alike, either. He had once tried to count the shades of orange, but at some imperceptible point the orange seemed to melt into yellow, and then within the yellow...Coryn's gizzard flinched. *A lovely shade of cream!* Soren was right — they were rushing into things. They should not be flying toward the canyonlands at all. They needed an immediate course correction. Coryn had only seen that peculiar cream color once before, and not in a fire but in the Beyond. It was on the glossy coat of a dire wolf. "Gyllbane!"

CHAPTER EIGHTEEN

Most Distressing News

It was a long way to the Beyond, but luckily once again the wind blew from behind and gave them a hefty push north and west. The night was thinning. The moon had slipped away into another world, and it was becoming that hazy time before the dawn. As they shifted positions in their flight formation so that Twilight could fly point in this murky light streaked with false shadows and blurred horizons, Soren could feel the tremor of excitement that coursed through their gizzards. They were at last to meet Gyllbane, the courageous she-wolf, who had turned on her own clan, the notorious MacHeaths, and befriended Coryn. Her own pup had been maimed by Lord MacHeath in hopes that this would qualify the young wolf to become a member of the Sacred Watch.

Once more, Soren felt a strange little ping in his gizzard. Otulissa! Had he dreamed of her? Had he seen something in a dream? Had his starsight revealed something he could not quite grasp? It seemed odd to him that now for the first time he was flying to the Beyond. Otulissa, of course, had been in the Beyond. That was where she had first found Coryn and taught him to collier and then ... *Well*, thought Soren, *as they say, the rest is history.*

"Fire in the sky! Volcanoes! Dead ahead!" Twilight shouted back.

The Band blinked as they perched atop a ridge. It was a strange and wonderful place, the Beyond. A trio of wolves approached them. The noble Gyllbane and her son, Cody, and the faithful Hamish, Coryn's best friend from his time in the Beyond. Hamish, born with a crippling deformity, had qualified for the Sacred Watch in which he had briefly served. But one of the true blessings of the ember was that once it was recovered, the wolves of the Watch were restored. What was broken in their bodies was mended. What was deformed was made to grow straight. What was crippled gained strength. When Coryn saw his dear friend Hamish come bounding up the rocky escarpment, sleek and powerful, he experienced an unspeakable thrill. And though he was far from the ember he felt a shimmering within him, a glow at the very core of his gizzard that he knew could only be that of the ember. It was strange, but for the first time he began to get a glimmering that one did not need to have the ember to possess it. He realized this as Hamish stepped closer and he touched his beak to Hamish's wet nose in greeting. Coryn saw the deep burnish of green in his wolf eyes, the same flickering green found in what they had come to think of as the gizzard of the Ember of Hoole. That glimpse of green in the wolf's eyes seemed to kindle a sympathetic response, a shimmering heat within Coryn.

Soren, although he had read about the wolf clans in the legends and heard from Coryn about their peculiar and elaborate codes of conduct, was nonetheless astonished. Despite Coryn's protests, the three wolves scraped the rough ground as they kneeled, then crouched and sunk to their bellies, twisting their necks in all sorts of odd contortions, then flattened their ears and flashing the whites of their eyes. This was the conduct required of a creature of low rank when approaching one of high rank. Coryn was a king and not for one minute would these wolves let him forget it.

After the introductions were made and the greetings exchanged, Gyllbane, one of the most beautiful wolves imaginable, turned to Coryn and said, "So, friend, what brings you here, so far from your island in the middle of the sea?"

Coryn turned his head toward the circle of the five volcanoes that made what was called the Sacred Ring. It all looked so different now. Colliers still plunged in steep dives to harvest the coal slopes that spilled from the volcanoes' craters, and there was the usual traffic on the fringes of the circle between the colliers and Rogue smiths as they haggled over the price of coals and whether one was truly bonk or not. But the immense piles of gnaw bones surrounding the five volcanoes seemed bare without the wolves of the watch keeping their vigil from the tops.

Finally, Coryn answered. "I began this journey for the most selfish of reasons. I feared that I bore the traces of a vile heritage. I could not put my obsession with my mother, Nyra, to rest."

Gyllbane blinked. In her own way, she understood this. She had met Nyra and knew her power, and she herself had once been a victim of ruthlessness. It had been hard for her to forget MacHeath and his abuse of her and her pup.

"And now?" Hamish asked. "Why have you come, old friend? Have you found out what you want to know?"

"Not really, but I have found out that she still lives and that in her possession is a book that is very dangerous. You've heard of hagsfiends?" The three wolves exchanged glances. Although it was fairly clear that the word was unfamiliar to them, they seemed disturbed. The hackles on the backs of their necks suddenly were erect, their eyes narrowed to green slits.

"Let us not talk out here. Follow me to my cave."

The cave shook with the thunderous eruptions of the volcanoes, and outside the night flinched with the red light of flames that scoured the sky. "And you say," Hamish spoke slowly, "that these creatures are no more?"

"Yes, they are extinct, yet not entirely gone," Gylfie said.

"I don't understand," Gyllbane said. "Either something is or it isn't, correct?"

Soren now spoke. "These hagsfiends that your ancestors — and ours — fought alongside Hoole, these creatures in their ancient forms are dead and gone. But they have left behind dim shadows. . . ." *How to explain it?* Soren thought. "Like whispers from another world they come to us, fragments from a bad dream. But it is not a dream. We have all had brushes with them. Haven't any of you dire wolves ever been haunted by such?"

Gyllbane shook her head. "Never. My old chief, MacHeath, was trouble enough. I surely didn't need a hagsfiend or even a dim shadow of one to cause more." Coryn felt a slight tremor reverberate in his gizzard when she spoke of the wrathful old wolf who had maimed her son, Cody, when he was just a pup. "What are these dim shadows of hagsfiends like?"

Soren continued. "Somewhat like scrooms, yet far less powerful." There was an undeniable nervous reaction among the three wolves in the cave when they heard this.

"We have not read the legends as you have and we need to know more about the ancient forms of the hags-fiends. Describe them to us." Then Gyllbane asked with a sudden urgency, "What do they look like, wherein lie their powers, and what exactly could they do to ordinary creatures?"

"You have to begin," Gylfie said, "with magen, for it was a time of magen in those ancient days — both good magen and evil magen." So Gylfie, the rest of the Band, and Coryn described as best they could what they had learned from reading the legends. But it was when they came to the peculiar yellow light that emanated from the hagsfiends' eyes that the three wolves stood up with every bit of their coats bristling, their eyes flashing white in a terror that Coryn had never in his time in the Beyond witnessed.

"Fyngrot, you call it?!" Gyllbane asked in a trembling voice.

"Yellow? Yellow pouring from their eyes?" Cody asked in nearly strangled words.

128

Soren explained in detail how the hagsfiends used fyngrot.

Hamish stepped forward. This time there were no gestures of homage. Rank was forgotten. "We have something similar among dire wolves. Vyrwolves," he said in a low growl. "We thought they were gone, too. A relic of our past, as I suppose you thought the hagsfiends were." A cold silence fell upon them all. *Great Glaux*, thought Soren, *can there be some connection between the two — between hagsfiends and vyrwolves?* Soren sensed that the same thought was occurring to Coryn. For indeed, once there had been a connection between the most evil wolf — MacHeath — and the most evil owl — Nyra.

"And they're not gone?" Coryn asked.

"We fear not," Gyllbane said.

"But I don't understand." Soren spoke now, his black eyes flickering with confusion. "How can they possibly be like hagsfiends? Wolves are not birds."

"Think of them as wingless hagsfiends." It was Digger who said this. They all spun their heads toward him and the three wolves regarded him with a measure of surprise.

"Precisely," Hamish said. "Wingless. But still very dangerous and sharing much in common with these hagsfiends that you described."

"This fyngrot," Gyllbane whispered tremulously. The incoherent roar of the erupting volcanoes mingled with the pounding of eight creatures' hearts. "It is like the jaunyx."

"The jaunyx?" the five owls asked in unison.

"Our eyes," Hamish said. "Our eyes are naturally green."

"A bright intense green, the same as the rim of the ember's center," Soren said.

The owls' gizzards were all astir now, for each one of them was remembering the passages from the legends in which King Hoole had, with the help of the bright beams from the wolves' eyes, broken through a powerful fyngrot and brought down a troop of hagsfiends in the Desert of Kuneer.

"They are still green," Gylfie whispered almost desperately. "Tell them, Soren, tell them of the passages from the legends where the wolves broke the fyngrot of the hagsfiends with the green of their eyes."

There was now a stirring among the wolves. They rose and turned in tight circles, then settled down again. "Is this true?" Gyllbane asked. "If so, we have lost this part of the tale as it was passed down since the first Fengo."

"Are legends true?" Soren asked no one in particular. "It was written down." He left the rest of what he was about to say unspoken. *But legends can inspire,* he thought. Soren knew that inspiration could not be told, or preached. It must be felt truly to be acted upon.

Gyllbane sighed. "Dunleavy MacHeath, the lord of my clan before I left it, his eyes began to fade soon after Coryn retrieved the coal." She paused.

"And?" Coryn asked.

Gyllbane turned toward her son. "Cody can tell you what happened."

"He'd always been a brute, Lord MacHeath. Thanks to him I am lame with two half paws, bitten off by my own chieftain in the hope that this would qualify me to become a gnaw wolf of the Sacred Watch."

"He lusted so for that ember, he maimed a defenseless pup," Gyllbane added, "just to be close to it. Then when the right owl came, he thought that owl would ..." Her voice dwindled off.

"And Nyra was the right owl," Coryn said.

"Yes, but you, Coryn, retrieved the ember instead," Cody continued. "For a while he thought all was lost. He became increasingly deranged and then fell into a distemper that was worse than the foaming disease. He staggered into the far southwestern range of hills and went deep into a cave somewhere there. For a long time we thought he had died. Many of the clan hoped and prayed and watched the spirit trail of stars that led to the soul cave where dead wolves go upon death, though few thought he deserved a place there. Then one day he came back with a new mate — Brygdylla. He looked ragged and his eyes had faded to almost no color — at least none that could be named. His new mate looked equally ragged and had the same colorless eyes. We thought she had suffered from the same illness. But then one night shortly after he had returned, he called a meeting of the clan in the Gadderheal. It was the night of a full moon, and he told us to follow him out of the Gadderheal cave and to stand across from him. As the moon rose and cast a perfect pool of silver light on the ground, he and Brygdylla stood in the center. A strange transformation began to occur."

There was a pause in the thunderous eruptions, and a quiet engulfed the cave that in its own way seemed as loud as the roar of the volcanoes. Cody continued. "MacHeath and his mate grew to three times their normal size, their dull, shaggy coats turned a dark glistening bluish-black, and their eyes were suddenly yellow. They pulled back their lips in a grimace not of fear but threat, revealing fangs — fangs the likes of which none of us had ever seen and twice their normal size, their edges no longer smooth but jagged with sharp little points."

"They had become vyrwolves," Hamish said. "And those MacHeaths who would not join them were slaughtered."

"But what about you, Cody? Why not you?"

"I never thought I would thank my lameness for this." He held up one of his mangled paws. "But since I'm maimed, I was of no use to them. Easily overlooked. And what was there to brag about in killing a maimed young wolf barely out of his puppy days?"

"And then what happened?" Soren asked. He did not like the sound of this at all. It had an eerie familiarity, a resonance with a dark legendary past. This must have been why Ezylryb had insisted on his deathbed that Soren, the Band, and the young king read the legends.

"And then MacHeath, Brygdylla, and a small remnant of the MacHeath clan — the ones he spared — went with him."

"But where?" Gylfie asked.

"To that cave in the southwestern hills."

"That cave!" Digger stepped forward. "I think I know of that cave." They all blinked and looked toward the Burrowing Owl.

"What?" Gylfie asked in a hoarse whisper.

"I think that cave leads to what is known among Burrowing Owls as the Tunnel of Despair." He paused. "A place where strange transformations took place. But none of us thought it was a real place. We thought —" He stopped, his voice almost broken. He peered down at his strong featherless legs, which had dug plenty of burrows and tunnels over the years in some of the hardest, most scrabbly earth imaginable. "We thought that it was just a mythical place, a legend." Digger paused, then began again. "But as we now know, legends have a way of revealing truth."

CHAPTER NINETEEN
An Owl with a Mission

How miserable can this get? Madame Plonk thought as icy slop from the Sea of Hoolemere dashed her in the face. She was wedged in between head-buffeting winds above and a tumultuous sea below. If she flew high to avoid the sea slop, the winds were too strong, at least for her, a frankly fat Snowy who had not been on a serious flight in years. Flying too low she encountered the rowdy breaking waves, which she felt took absolute delight in drenching her. Madame Plonk had to admit she was definitely out of shape. But she flew on. She had gotten Otulissa into this mess back at the tree and she would get her out of it. She felt terrible about asking Otulissa to hide the frinkin' coronation teacup, which she hoped she never laid eyes on again. But most of all she felt deeply ashamed for ever partaking of, and lending her voice, her most precious possession, to these yoickish rituals dreamed up by the GGE. She was as fed up with the frinkin' ember as she was with the teacup.

All these thoughts assailed her as she flew on. Despite her vanity and frivolous habits, she was in many ways a practical owl. She knew that it would do her no good to dwell on the past. She must not squander her strength, but conserve it and fly on. A fuzzy line began to break through the thick vapors of mist and fog and spume-tossed air. *Land!* she thought. Then the fuzzy line grew bolder and assumed a shape. *It must be Cape Glaux.* She hadn't seen it in years and although it was a barren windswept promontory, to Madame Plonk it seemed like the most welcoming place in the world. She would only allow herself a short rest, for night was now falling and to fly in the daylight would be dangerous. Crows! How long had it been since she even had to consider the foul creatures? But it wouldn't do to become the victim of a mobbing. She had to find Soren, the Band, and the young king. Bubo had told her the whereabouts of a grog tree. "When you get to the Cape, fly off the bottom port star of the Golden Talons, not the starboard star."

"Port? Starboard? What do I know of such things? Tell me plain, Bubo," she had demanded.

"All right. Go to the Cape, turn left, fly straight for two hours. You'll get to Silverveil, and that forest on its far western side meets up with the Shadow Forest. If you fly a straight course, on the border between the two forests you'll find the grog tree in a stand of sycamores."

She was absolutely starving by the time she arrived on the Cape, and luckily a rock rat was perched almost smack dab beneath her in a thicket of coarse winter grass. She looked about for a tree and a hollow even though she knew it was foolish, but it had been so long since she had holed up in a ground scrape, although this was the customary shelter of her kind. She had grown accustomed to more luxuriously appointed residences during her time at the tree. Indeed, she did not even call her hollow a hollow but an apartment and had lined it with the plushest of mosses, and all manner of decorations she had acquired through her dealings with Trader Mags.

"Aaah, dear Mags!" She realized that she would be flying right through Mags' home territory in Silverveil. How she would love . . . She cut off the thought almost immediately. *How can I be thinking about shopping at a time like this?!* She gave herself a stern talking-to: "Time to shape up, old gal! You're on a mission. You sybaritic hunk of feathers, you gluttonous, high-living lowlife of a fat owl." She looked down at the rock rat she had just killed and felt her hunger vanish. *Well, maybe I'll get thin.* But she knew she had to eat something, for soon she would have to fly on. Not a drop of the night could be wasted. She tore off the rat's head, then swallowed the rest. Normally, she would have eaten the head but she knew there was little nutritional value in it, so why take on the extra weight? It would only make flying into a headwind — *Pardon the pun,* she thought — more difficult. For exactly five seconds she felt proud of her willpower, but she suddenly burst into tears. "I'm such a fool, a vain old fool." She crammed herself into a shallow ground scrape beneath a rock shelf overhang, collapsed in an exhausted heap, and instantly fell sound asleep.

Madame Plonk was dreaming of bars, vertical iron bars, and behind them the dignified face of a Spotted Owl. "Sorry! So sorry! Stupid teacup!" Her own sobbing woke her up and then her eyes flinched in the blinding white light. "Great Glaux, I've slept into the day! How could I! How could I!" She was hysterical now. She would have to wait until night, and even though these winter days were short, any delay was risky not just to the well-being of Otulissa but of the entire tree. The Band had to come back as quickly as possible. Shaking and awash with a mix of anger at herself and fear, she was dissolving into a complete panic. The glare of the sun was a scorching mockery. But through her panic she saw something even whiter than the sun. Whiter than the sun but with a sudden dash of black, a black that looked rather crowish . . .

Oh, great Glaux! I'm done for! she screeched, and swooned, collapsing, in a heap.

Madame Plonk was not sure how long she was out, but when she came to an astonishing sight met her eyes. It was a Snowy bending over her: a large male, pure white except for a black feather tucked into the plumage behind his head. *How very odd.* Madame Plonk blinked.

"Madame, may I be of service? You seem most distressed." It was a gentleman speaking, no doubt about that, Madame Plonk thought. She tried to compose herself before she spoke. "I was having a bad dream," she began and then blurted out, "but I deserve it. I'm a terrible owl. I have done a terrible thing!"

"Now, now, madame, I'm sure it can't be all that bad."

"Oh, but it is!" Between sobs and gulps, Madame Plonk spilled out her story. It was a jumbled tale of teacups, ashes, cracked voices, a Spotted Owl named Otulissa, and Coryn.

"Coryn!" the male Snowy exclaimed.

"Yes, Coryn, the king of the great tree."

"So that is where you are from."

Madame Plonk nodded.

"You must be the famed singer of the tree."

"Once," she replied cryptically.

He blinked, not quite understanding her, but went on. "Oh, yes, I know about you and the great tree and the new king, Coryn." He paused. "You see, I knew him when he was still called Nyroc."

"You did?" Madame Plonk blinked.

"Well, I am rather ashamed of how I came to know him, but yes, I did make his acquaintance briefly."

"I must find him. I must find him and the Band."

"Oh, you shall, Madame Plonk. You see you have come upon the right owl. I am Doc Finebeak, the finest tracker in the Southern Kingdoms. Once upon a time, I was hired by Nyra to track down her errant son. I know this young owl. I know his flight track. If anyone can find him and this Band you speak of, it's me. We can leave immediately."

"What? It's broad daylight. Are you yoicks? What about crows?"

"What about crows?" He cocked his head so that the black feather showed. "The crows and I, well, how shall I put it? The crows and I have an arrangement. This crow feather I wear — it's a long story how I got it, but basically it gives me a free passage for daytime flight — a get-out-of-mobbing-free feather, so to speak."

"Oh . . ." That was all Madame Plonk could say. Just "oh" and deep in her chest she felt a shimmering flutter in her gizzard. She hadn't felt that in years! *My, my! I mustn't be distracted. Just think* mission, *you old fool!*

CHAPTER TWENTY
The Tunnel of Despair

Gylfie was chosen for the mission of exploring the Tunnel of Despair for two reasons. First, she was small and could thread her way undetected through the bizarre underground twisting channel that sometimes narrowed to the width of a Barn Owl's wingspan; second, she was the premier navigator of the great tree. Of any of them, she would never get lost. Take away every starry reference point, take away the sky, as indeed was the case, and it mattered not to Gylfie.

Stone flowers bloomed in the dense shadows as Gylfie flew through the twisting maze of passages. A lesser owl, one of inferior intelligence or unsteady gizzard, might have found these weird contortions of rock frightening. They seemed to grow magically from the floor, ceiling, and sides of the tunnel in myriad shapes ranging from needlelike protuberances to blossoms locked in an eternal spring. But Gylfie was no lesser owl. Her mind buzzed with star charts and the configurations of the constellations in the sky above. Her brain and gizzard tingled with the minute vibrations of the Earth's magnetic poles. Within her were both chart and compass.

Still, Gylfie was not used to being underground. Although she was flying, she felt as if she were being buried alive because with each wing beat she was moving deeper into the Earth. *Earth is not a place for a winged creature,* she thought. The damp smell of clay, rock, and soil offended her sensibilities. She hated not seeing the sky. That's how it had been at St. Aggie's when they were imprisoned deep in the stone maze, exposed to the full shine of the moon for moon blinking. She felt her gizzard grow squishy with dread and her heartbeat accelerate. *Keep calm! Keep calm! The sky is there. You just can't see it. I've had worse experiences — like when I was captured by kraals in the Northern Kingdoms. I have to do this for the Band. For the tree. For owlkind, birdkind, animalkind. Don't be some weak-gizzard moon calf, freak gizzle, idiotic owl.* Gylfie kept up the self-scolding. She would fly on. She had flown in battle, through hurricanes, and through fires. She could fly through this frinkin' stupid tunnel!

The only other owl of the Band who would have possibly been adequate for the job, despite his lack of celestial navigation abilities, was Digger. As a Burrowing Owl he had an extensive knowledge of caves and tunnels and the topography of the underground; not only the topography but the cave dwellers, the peculiar animals that lived in caves. But with a wingspan of nearly two feet, Digger was too big. He told Gylfie as much as he could about the natural history of caves and tunnels in general. However there was not much time. For the moon had long passed its dwenking and was well into its newing, growing fatter and fatter each night. The strange transformation of the dire wolves into vyrwolves took place, they had been told, on the night of a full moon. But even before they were told this, Coryn had been nervous about the newing moon because this time there would be an eclipse. Coryn's words now flowed back to Gylfie as she flew the twisting channels of the earth: "*Do you know the significance of an eclipse?*" Coryn had asked with a quaver in his voice.

Neither Coryn nor the Band had known that at the very same moment he had spoken these words, his own mother was speaking nearly the same words to Stryker, her top lieutenant. Still, Coryn's obvious agitation over the coming eclipse coupled with what they now knew of the effect of the full moon on vyrwolves added an acute urgency to her mission.

Aside from the navigational information Gylfie was continuously processing as she flew, she kept in mind Digger's stories of the tunnel. The legend of the place interlocked with its natural history in a remarkable manner. The tunnel, which meandered off into caves of varying sizes, was perforated with thousands of holes, cracks, and crevices through which rainwater seeped. On its journey downward, this water dissolved the rock in its path, leaving these many cave flowers and strange formations. And as the water collected, it turned fizzy and bubbled not with heat but odd gases. The oldest caves and pools were closest to the Earth's surface. As water continued to leak down, cutting more passageways, the newer caverns were formed. It was in the oldest caves, however, with their burbling gaseous pools, that strange creatures lived. Eyeless fish and shrimp, blind albino crayfish, and all manner of strange spiders. Certain kinds of eels and catfish also found their way from aboveground streams into those of the Tunnel of Despair. And finally there were trogloxenes — cave visitors or cave guests — crickets, bats, rats, and flying insects, and, Gylfie supposed, herself. There was in the Tunnel of Despair an unnatural history as well and it, too, had its source in the pools and lakes. For it was the deep water of certain pools that gave rise to vyrwolves. By drinking deeply from these pools, a wolf — not an ordinary wolf but a vicious or depraved one with a touch of evil — could be transformed into a wolf with the potential for extraordinary evil, and on nights of the full moon become a vyrwolf.

Gylfie's mission was to find any trace of these wolves and to locate this pool of potent waters. She was also to explore and see where the tunnel ended. Coryn knew that Nyra had collaborated with MacHeath to try to seize the ember. If they were together again, the destruction they could wreak was gizzard-freezing, unthinkable. With the full moon and its eclipse fast approaching, it was as if heaven and earth were conspiring to inexorably arrange themselves in a deadly design. A dance of death was about to commence.

Gylfie was not sure how long she had been flying, but she knew she had covered several leagues with all the twists and turns. She had rarely stopped to rest, but now just ahead there was a welcoming niche and she thought she would fetch up in it. The tunnel, of course, was windless and Gylfie had never felt more cut off from all the things that had meaning for an owl — the billowing thermal drafts of air rising from earth warmed by the sun, the coolness of the night, the moon scattering its silver on her wings, the stars — the dear, dear stars in their familiar transits across the velvet of the night. She slipped into the niche. A flatworm was crawling by and she peeled him off the stone ledge with her tiny talons and popped him in her mouth, then settled in for a short snooze.

It was the smell that first woke her — deeply rank, wet, wet fur! *And they say owls can't smell!* And then she became aware of a loud panting. *I'm near!* she thought. She shut her eyes tight and told herself not to panic. *I must stay calm. I must find out as much as I can.* She stepped out onto the ledge. Her talons clicked against the stone. She froze. She would have to fly. And she wasn't the most silent of fliers. Still, it would be more silent than trying to creep up on them with her talons striking the rock surfaces. She flew close to the wall. Suddenly, there was light! Gylfie blinked. A moon hung in the darkness of the tunnel. For a second she felt completely disoriented and faltered in flight, recovering just before colliding with a stone flower. She lighted down. *The moon? Impossible!*

And then she realized that through an opening in the cave's roof the moon was reflected in a large pool of water. Still water. All the pools she had seen so far were fizzing with tiny bubbles, but not this one. And it was not only the moon she saw reflected in its dark surface but the faces of a half dozen wolves.

"Drink, drink deeply," one wolf counseled. "It has been a whole moon cycle since last we met to drink of the vyr. Our strength has waned but it will come back. Yes, it will!" As the wolf said this, he lifted his head and swung it in Gylfie's direction. His eyes hung in the blackness like two yellow flames. Gylfie felt a coldness in her gizzard. Her wings drooped. It was like every fyngrot she had imagined when they had read the legends. This was a hag-wolf if there ever was one. She wilfed and grew thinner. She heard in the distance a fluttering of wings, large wings. And then there was a second moon! A scarred moon. There was only one owl with such a face. Nyra!

CHAPTER TWENTY-ONE

Race the Moon

So you're sure, Gylfie, that the cave over there is where you would have emerged if you had been able to go to the very end of the tunnel?" Soren cocked his head in the direction to which he was referring. The owls had flown to the canyonlands as soon as Gylfie had reported back to them at their prearranged meeting place in the Shadow Forest.

"Absolutely." The tiny Elf Owl nodded firmly. "Somehow I managed to fly out of it while the wolves were still drinking at that pool just before the tunnel widened into the cave. No one saw me."

"And this is the cave of Kludd's Final ceremony?" Twilight looked at Coryn.

"It is. And just over there in those cliffs beyond the next ridge is the stone hollow where I was raised." Coryn swiveled his head around. This place was filled with bad memories. His First Flight ceremony. His mother's rage, his own despair over his friend Phillip, the terrible fear when he had experienced his first visions in the fires of his father's Final ceremony and realized that he had been lied to since the moment of his hatching.

It seemed an uncanny twist of fate that the Tunnel of Despair had ended in the very same cave in which Kludd had been killed. The Band, Coryn, Gyllbane, and the other wolves who traveled with her were gathered on a ridge in the canyonlands. Gyllbane and the wolves she could muster had traveled in a byrrgis at a speed they called "press paw"— not as fast as attack or chase speed but fast enough to cover long distances quickly.

It had been hard to get more wolves, for it was mating season and the clans were scattered. But Hamish had known where to find Duncan MacDuncan and his lieutenant. Gyllbane had prevailed upon Fitzmore McFang, who had kindly taken her in after she had left the MacHeaths. McFang had come with his powerful mate, Adair, who was as fearless as she was strong. Their son, Fitzy, had also come. In addition to these, there were three from the MacNamara clan, a clan traditionally headed up by a female always called Namara. And because MacNamara she-wolves were known for their toughness and great intelligence, males vied for them. But only one male would be chosen and, contrary to all custom, he would drop his birth clan name and assume that of

MacNamara. So Namara came with her mate Cormag and their son, Airilla, and daughter, Morag. In all, there were a dozen wolves. But they were dire wolves — not vyrwolves. It remained to be seen if it would be an even match.

"Are the vyrwolves all in the cave now?" Twilight whispered.

"I think so," Namara answered. She lifted her nose. "The scent marks are old out here. They have not been out for some time."

The owls and the wolves knew that they had to strike before the moon rose, but cave battles were difficult. Even in a large cave, space would be tight if they fought with fire. And they did plan to do just that. There were other considerations that made the cave far from ideal: It led into a long, long tunnel. The last thing they wanted was for the vyrwolves to scatter down the intricate maze of passages. They had to assume that the vyrwolves and Nyra and her remnant Pure Ones knew the terrain of the tunnel better than they did. That meant that Nyra and the wolves would be fighting on familiar territory. This would give them a distinct advantage. But if they rushed them in the cave — before the moonlight shone on them — the wolves would still be just wolves and not vyrwolves. For that transformation, they needed to expose themselves to the moon. It was a very hard call to make.

*   *   *

They say owls can't smell, Stryker thought to himself. But he could. He could smell the fetid stink of these wolves to whom his commander, General Mam, had allied them. There was no choice, really. Their own ranks had been shattered, and he had to admit these wolves had powers — powers that Nyra felt were akin in some mysterious ways to the powers that she hoped to attain. She was saying the words again now.

"The book, the transforming waters, these ashes of my dear Kludd." She ran her beak through the ashes and seemed to inhale them as if savoring their scent. "These ashes, my friends" — she swiveled her head to look at the congregation of wolves and remaining Pure Ones — "are the key to what the ancients called nachtmagen. With them, you will see, I shall transform my son — and, with that, the ember shall be ours. "

"Does the book say that, General Mam?" Stryker asked.

"You doubt me, Stryker?" It was as if a stream of yellow heat glared from Nyra's eyes.

"Never, my general." He raised his right talon in the salute that Nyra had recently begun insisting upon when being addressed. It seemed that since their numbers had been depleted, Nyra had become increasingly obsesssed with these formal gestures indicating acknowledgment of her exalted state. She greatly admired the elaborate codes of conduct that the wolves required between the lower and the higher ranks and wished that owls could scrape the ground as effectively as the wolves did when they cowered on their bellies in front of MacHeath, rolling their eyes back until they flashed white. But this was simply not how owls were constructed.

She lowered her voice and spoke in a close, intimate tone. "You see, my dear Stryker, I feel a kinship with this ancient bird named Kreeth." She would not admit that the words from the book were hard for her to read. The diagrams and the pictures were really enough. She sensed their meaning. "I understand the science of nachtmagen. These are deep things that only a chosen few can comprehend. And Kreeth and I are among them. Or she was . . ."

Stryker, though not very bright, was mulling over some troubling thoughts. The Pure Ones' entire philosophy was based upon Barn Owls being the most superior breed of all owls. And yet this Kreeth was not even a true owl. She was a hagsfiend, a strange cross between owl and crow. He himself had encountered those ragtag remnants that came like dark wisps of bad dreams as one flew through the night. Their hauntings, although startling, were harmless. But here was Nyra, claiming kinship with an archfiend from some distant past who was as far from pure as one could imagine. He dared not question her, though. No, never. He regarded her now, as she once again ran her beak through the ashes, and observed that there seemed to be a darkening of the white feathers at the edges of her face.

Always just before a battle there were those quiet thoughts one had — random notions that often had nothing to do with the attack, with strategy, or even with premonitions of death. Soren was experiencing such thoughts as he perched on the ridge and swiveled his head toward his nephew. Coryn appeared to almost bristle with readiness and gallgrot for this fight. But would he be strong enough to face his mother? To fight her to the death if need be? To kill her? Soren vowed that he would spare Coryn that horrendous task. He would kill Nyra. A son, even the son of one as terrible as Nyra, should not be required to fight his mother to the death.

How odd, Soren thought, that it had been his intention to set out on this journey with his nephew to distract him from his obsession with Nyra and his own haggishness. Instead he must face her. Then for perhaps the thousandth time, Soren wished that Otulissa were here. The Spotted Owl was a superb strategist. He closed his eyes and tried to think of how she would have planned the attack. Once again he felt that deep twinge in his gizzard. *Why is it that every time I think of Otulissa I feel something like dread?*

It was a race with the moon. When the wolves came out under the full-shine moonlight they would become monsters. But with the eclipse, would they lose their power or would a worse one arise? If Soren could have flown up and stopped the moon he would have. He looked up and blinked at it. Two great forces were coming together on their inevitable course. Would he try if he could to stop the moon or stop the Earth? Stay the night or wish for the day? For it was the night of a lunar eclipse when the Earth in its orbit would come between the moon and the sun. He imagined that first bite that the Earth's shadow would take from the moon as the eclipse began. He imagined . . . and in that instant his dream came back. The slits in the ether veil! The black feathers piercing through. *"Don't wait for me!"* That voice — it was Otulissa's! *"Go! Go!"*

Soren turned to Coryn. "We go now!" Behind them in a shallow trough in the rocks were dozens of smoldering coals. Nearby were neatly stacked dried twigs and limbs gathered from the Shadow Forest. When Gylfie had met up with the Band and the wolves in the Shadow Forest and given her report, with the help of the wolves the owls had begun to gather their arsenal, for they knew that trees were sparse in the canyonlands, especially since the Battle of the Great Burning. From the Beyond they had brought coals in their botkins and buckets.

Coryn watched nervously as the Band chose their weapons — two light spruce twigs with fine tufts of needles on their tips for Gylfie; a larger limb for Twilight, who could handle the heft of the well-seasoned oak branch that would burn slowly and maintain a glowing, fiery tip. Soren chose a pliant limb from a fir tree. He knew firs, and this particular limb had an abundance of needle clusters. It would be the most strategic weapon of all. With his superb flying skills, Soren would be able to clear a path as if he were brandishing a comet. Digger, who had the strongest legs of any of them, would carry a double-fired birch limb. With flames at each end of the branch, he would grip the limb from the middle and wield it like a stave. After selecting the right weapon, with a near ritualistic serenity each owl would dip it into the coals to ignite it. The Band had all been tested in battle. But Coryn, though he had survived more than his fair share of tests of courage, had never really been tried in full battle. And although he was perhaps one of the greatest colliers who ever lived he had never fought with fire. How the young king envied the four owls of the Band their confidence, their single-mindedness, their unswerving determination. From the smallest to the largest, they seemed so resolute, so ready. And yet who had more at stake than himself? He was about to face the mother who once tried to kill him. He was the king of the Great Ga'Hoole Tree. But did he have Ga', that elusive spirit he had read about in the legends? Hoole's mother, Queen Siv, was said to have had it. Coryn suspected that his uncle Soren possessed Ga'. He looked at his uncle now as he stepped forward to ignite his branch. Coryn would be next. Would something fire within him to steady his nerves, to trim his gizzard for this battle? Yes, he had retrieved the ember, but did he have Ga'? That was the question.

CHAPTER TWENTY-TWO

The Book, the Battle, and the Band

There were two thoughts in their minds as they flew with their burning branches toward the cave: Don't let the wolves or Nyra leave the cave and don't let them go deeper into the tunnel. That was their strategy, coupled with the element of surprise. There was one other thing that they had to accomplish, and indeed, this was the entire purpose of the attack: to take *The Book of Kreeth*. Gylfie had managed to see where Nyra had put the book. It was in a niche just above the fire pit where Kludd's bones had been burned. The ashes of those bones were still there in a small pile encircled by stones — an altar to a tyrant.

And now, deep in the bowels of the earth, Nyra perched near the tyrant's ashes, hoping with Kreeth's book of charms and spells, to re-create herself as a hags-fiend and ultimately regain and re-create her son. And then — *the ember*.

Outside the cave the twelve wolves were crouching on top of boulders, ready to pounce should a vyrwolf charge from the cave. The Band had remembered how in the legends Hoole had used the wolves and the intense green light of their eyes to cut through the fyngrot of the hagsfiends. If the wolves in the cave escaped into the light of the full moon, could this weapon of green light be used now? Would it work? They all hoped that there would be no need to find out, that the vyrwolves would be contained within the cave and be brought to a quick end.

The moon was slipping up over the horizon in its unstoppable ascent. Another thought flitted through the minds of both Soren and Gylfie. How deadly the moon could be! Years before as near hatchlings — when they were both imprisoned not far from this very spot in the canyonlands in St. Aggie's — they had been forced to remain under the light of the full moon as part of those tyrannical owls' attempts to moon blink them. Somehow they had survived and now the memory emboldened them.

"Hi-yiiiiii!!" Soren gave the shrill shriek of a Barn Owl as he whizzed into the cave with his burning firebrand. A fiery blizzard of sparks crackled through the darkness. He flew in steep, ascending and plunging loops until the cave was crisscrossed with trails of sparks. The wolves began to howl. Nyra and her owls screeched and flew for their battle claws.

Under the cover of this fiery melee, Gylfie flew with two ignited spruce twigs, one in each talon. *Steady, steady,* she told herself as directly ahead she saw a wolf's jaw drop, opening a pink cavern that could easily swallow her whole. She flew right for the throat and crammed one of her flaming twigs down the wolf's gullet. A tremendous gagging howl ripped through the cave. One twig gone but she still had one left. She wheeled around and saw Nyra come toward her. Nyra had only had time to put on one battle claw. It shot out toward Gylfie, but it merely raked the air as Gylfie darted out of Nyra's path. Because of the single battle claw Nyra was flying unbalanced. Gylfie realized that this was to her own advantage. She must continue to distract Nyra by leading her away from the niche where the book was hidden. It was Cody's job to retrieve the book. With her remaining twig, Gylfie feinted and jabbed at Nyra, who was maddened by the little owl. She then wheeled around to come in for a new, angled attack. That was when Nyra spotted Coryn. He was backing a snarling wolf into a corner with a double-fired branch similar to Digger's.

"You!" Nyra screeched.

And then a searing taunt seized the air. It was Twilight bellowing at the top of his lungs.

> *General Mam, she don't scare me,*
> *she ain't gonna make me flee.*
> *General Mam, she so dumb,*
> *she don't know which way to run.*
> *Fly by night, fly by day —*
> *she ain't gonna get away.*
> *She so ugly, that frinkin' face,*
> *she ain't nothing but a fat disgrace.*
> *Disgrace in word, disgrace in deed,*
> *Monster Mam is what I see!*

Nyra staggered in flight, then tore off her battle claw and, seizing it like a flail, began to swing it wildly at Twilight. Suddenly, blood and sparks flew through the air. Twilight began to plummet. "No!" An anguished cry tore through the cave.

"Yes! The mighty Twilight falls!" Nyra screeched. There was a blur as Nyra flew toward the back of the cave. "Death to Twilight, killer of Kludd!"

"Stop her!" someone cried out.

The Tunnel, the Tunnel of Despair. They can't go in! That was all that Digger could think of as he tried, with his double-fired staves, to block the part of the cave that led into the tunnel. Digger was quick but not quick enough. Nyra slipped by him and now three wolves were charging him. He clipped one, setting its tail on fire. But he knew he had failed to block the tunnel.

"I'm after them!" Coryn shouted as he flew by with his fir branch spitting fire.

Furious, Digger cracked his long stave on a sharp edge of a rock, splitting it in half so he could fly down the narrow passageways of the tunnel. He had to go. Despite their narrowness, he knew best how to navigate the twisting channels of the cave. Gylfie had been there before, of course, but she was occupied with helping Cody retrieve the book. So he flew in the wake of Coryn, a burning stump of stave in each talon. The defense of blocking the tunnel entrance had failed. This was a battle that was going to be carried deep into the earth.

But perhaps not deep enough. Through a slit in the rock, a filament of moonlight seeped, a sliver of light no bigger than the thread of a plummel.

CHAPTER TWENTY-THREE

Mysticus!

S trange!" Doc Finebeak muttered as he alighted on a rock outcropping a short distance from the cave where the fighting had erupted.

"What?" Madame Plonk asked.

"I had the trail. I mean, we're still on their track but I get the oddest feeling that it has doubled back . . . back to where we are right here."

"But how could that be?" Madame Plonk hesitated. She was not sure exactly how to address this handsome, distinguished Snowy. They had been flying together for more than two nights. To call him Doc Finebeak seemed rather formal, and also was a beakful. He had not given her any other name, however. "Doc" seemed too casual. Beakie? Too familiar. Madame Plonk blinked and blinked again. Something was visible above a depression in the very rugged terrain not far ahead. "What in the world is that?" she whispered. In the light of the moon, two bright yellow slashes seemed to float just above the ground.

They rose and winged cautiously closer.

"It's . . . it's . . ." Doc Finebeak hesitated, then whispered, "a wolf!" There was more movement close to the ground and then a plume of sparks. *A volcano, here?* Finebeak wondered. It was not a volcano, but the earth seemed to be erupting. Sparks, wolves, and owls spouted from the ground. "A cave battle!" Doc Finebeak exclaimed. Some owls were fighting each other with burning branches, some were chasing the wolves and were brandishing fire as well. The battle was both above and below ground now.

"It's Coryn!" Madame Plonk gasped. "Coryn, our king." They watched in stunned silence. But now something even more peculiar was happening. Some of the wolves stopped fighting and were gamboling in the moonlight. They were growing larger before Madame Plonk's and Doc Finebeak's very eyes. They were becoming enormous.

"Great Glaux!" Madame Plonk exclaimed.

"They need our help!" Doc Finebak said. Four simple little words, but nearly incomprehensible to Madame Plonk. *What?* What in the world could she possibly do in a situation like this? *Me, fight? Fight with fire? Fight with anything?*

Ahead of them two Barn Owls rose higher, above the fray — Nyra and Coryn.

Doc Finebeak roared, spread his great wings even

wider and powered forward. "I let this female almost kill her own son once. I shall not stand by this time! Never again!"

Me? Madame Plonk thought desperately again. Panic welled in the back of her throat. *I'm a fat owl with a cracked voice.* She opened her beak to protest her helplessness. And from it a note came pealing into the night. Madame Plonk had sung many high notes before in her life. High C was an ordinary vocal experience for the singer of the great tree but right now in this moment, under the full moon with the shadow of the Earth creeping in front of it, she hit an unbelievable note. It was not simply high C. It was C-sharp in the eighth octave, the note sometimes referred to by other singers as *mysticus*. High enough to shatter glass. And now its vibrations shimmered out into the night. The wolves who had been yelping and howling fell to the ground writhing in pain. Chips of mica split off rocks. But the moon was not stayed.

Digger flew up. "Plonk, keep singing, but go to Twilight. He's . . . he's dying."

"What!" she shreed, and a vyrwolf fell dead. Gyllbane and her pack fought on and above the writhing vyrwolves, who seemed vastly more affected by the mysticus than the dire wolves, Coryn and Nyra began to circle each other in flight. The merest sliver of the moon disappeared as the shadow of the Earth began to slide across it. Nyra swung her head toward her son and hissed. "We belong together, Nyroc. We were both hatched on a night such as this. Our power is great and will become greater tonight."

"That is no longer my name. I am Coryn."

"You are Nyroc and you are nothing without me." The night was growing dimmer as the Earth's shadow ate away at the moon, gnawing it like a fanged animal tearing flesh from bone. Nyra held the single battle claw in her two talons, and Coryn knew she could swing and attack with great accuracy. He still had the drops of Twilight's blood splattered on his face, and he would never forget the sight of the Great Gray plummeting in a fiery red rain of blood and sparks. Coryn's own double-fired branch was losing its heat. One end was nearly extinguished. If only the wind would rise and breathe some life into the remaining fire. *If only . . . my life is filled with "if onlys."*

Suddenly, Nyra was nearly upon him. She now had the battle claw in her teeth and a flaming branch in her talons. She was advancing upon him, pressing him against a sheer cliff wall. He hovered, backstroking as she continued to advance. He could feel his tail feathers graze the wall. He was alone. There was no Twilight to begin a taunting chant. Where was Soren? That excruciatingly high note continued to scratch the night and the flames of Nyra's branch were singeing his breast feathers. He could feel their heat. But it was not the heat of flame he felt. What heat was that? It was coming from within him. His gizzard felt on fire.

Nyra suddenly stopped advancing. She blinked. *What is this?* she thought. *My son's eyes are burning green, green like those of a wolf, but not a vyrwolf.* The light flowing like a liquid green flame from Coryn's eyes was overpowering. Deep within that light was a flicker of orange with a lick of blue at its center. But the mysterious light was coming from that ring of green. The orange, the blue, the green — was not that like the Ember of Hoole? Coryn saw Nyra begin to go yeep. Yet he hardly noticed. He just felt this overpowering glow within him. *Impossible,* he thought. He was here and the ember was far away.

The world went black and silence filled the night. The singing stopped. Coryn looked around. There was no one. Nyra had vanished. She was not on the ground or in the air. He flew down to have a closer look. No sign of her. In the back of his mind, there was a fleeting thought: Could she have fallen into one of the openings of the Tunnel of Despair? The wolves, too, seemed to have vanished. Were they in the tunnel as well? Had the earth opened to swallow this evil? *May it stay in the tunnel forever,* he thought. In the distance close to the ground, Coryn glimpsed a puff of white. He flew toward it. As he flew, he noticed beneath him a carnage of wolves, but so far no bodies of owls, and although he did not recognize the wolves as the ones who had come with them from the Beyond, they certainly did not look like vyrwolves. They were of normal size, their different colors ranging from gray to brown to cream. Was this like that desert battle of the hagsfiends he had read about in the legends when the hagsfiends, finally vanquished, looked no bigger than ordinary crows? As he drew closer, his gizzard stilled. Something awful was ahead. His mind, his heart, his gizzard railed against it. *No, not Twilight. Not Twilight . . .*

CHAPTER TWENTY-FOUR

Not Twilight

It wasn't Twilight. It was Cody. Gyllbane's sobs racked the night. The young wolf barely beyond being pup lay atop *The Book of Kreeth*, his throat slashed. "He saved the book," Gyllbane sobbed. "He saved it, but for what?" She raised her head. Coryn's gizzard was wrenched. Here was a mother who truly loved her son.

Near Cody's body lay Twilight. Madame Plonk was hovering over him, fanning him with her large wings. The Band crowded in close. He had lost a great deal of blood. He seemed shrunken and his gaze wandered deliriously.

"How will we ever get him back to the great tree?" Coryn asked.

"We won't," said Digger solemnly. Coryn blinked. Was Digger saying that Twilight would die here? He didn't understand. This wasn't like the Band. Not at all like the Band — and where was Soren?

"Where's Soren? He isn't hurt, is he?"

"No." Gylfie stepped forward. "Soren is on his way to

Ambala with Doc Finebeak. They will fly through the rest of the night and through the day."

"Why?" asked Coryn. But the rest of them really weren't hearing Coryn's questions. They were all staring at his eyes as the last telltale reflections of the Ember of Hoole faded from them. "Why?" demanded Coryn more forcefully. "Why, at a time like this, is he flying to Ambala?"

Gylfie stepped forward closer now and looked up into the young king's eyes, still searching for what she thought she had glimpsed. "He has gone to Ambala to seek Slynella and Stingyll."

"Slynella and Stingyll!" Coryn felt his gizzard stir with happiness because these were the two flying snakes, companions of Mist, who lived with her in the eagle's nest high in the mountaintops of Ambala. Their poisonous venom could also cure, if properly dispensed from the two prongs of their ivory-and-crimson forked tongues. The snakes had befriended Coryn after he had left his mother and the Pure Ones, when Coryn had been treated as an outcast and forced to flee nearly every forest in the Southern Kingdoms.

If only Twilight could live until they arrived. Soren was a fast flier, and with Doc Finebeak's free pass through crow territory, perhaps there was a chance. Coryn crouched down on the ground near the Great Gray.

"Twilight," Coryn whispered. "Live. Please live." The other owls huddled in closer. They, too, began to speak encouraging words despite their worst fears. Gylfie and Digger were dazed. They had been the Band forever. They had been four. *And now with Twilight on the brink of death, and Soren away, we feel* . . . Gylfie thought, *like an owl with one wing. Halved. Diminished.*

For the rest of the night and through the next day they all spoke encouraging words to the Great Gray, and Madame Plonk continued to fan Twilight tirelessly with her enormous white wings. A vole was caught, killed, and its blood squeezed into Twilight's parched throat. Twilight had been thrashing and restless, but now as tween time approached, he grew quieter. Digger and Gylfie and Madame Plonk glanced nervously at one another. What did this mean? They all knew this was the hour that Twilight had been named for. It was that silvery edge of time that truly was Twilight's hour. He was an owl who could see things that other birds could not when the boundaries between day and night became dim and shapes melted away, when the edges of time and space, of earth and sky, became uncertain. How often had they heard the Great Gray say, "I live on the edge and I love it"? But what edge was that dear, brash owl teetering on now?

Was it truly the edge between being and not being, between sky and glaumora, between life and death? For Twilight to die at twilight, for him to draw his last breath as the evening shadows gathered seemed so wrong.

So very wrong, Gylfie thought.

"Look!" Hamish said. "Look to the east." Two glowing scrolls of green unfurled through a low-flying cloud.

"It's Slynella!" Gylfie shrieked.

"And Stingyll!" Digger gasped in relief. The two flying snakes were flanked by Soren and Doc Finebeak.

"Hang on!" Gylfie crouched close to Twilight's ear slits. "Hang on! Remember how they saved Soren that time, Twilight?"

The venomous green flying snakes of Ambala, elixirs for life and poisons for death in their forked tongues, could cure the most grievously wounded, but they could not bring back the dead. Gylfie glanced at Gyllbane, who had dragged herself to her feet and looked longingly as the snakes coiled themselves around the barely breathing body of Twilight. Gylfie flew back and lighted down in the ruff of Gyllbane's neck fur. "I am so sorry, Gyllbane. So very sorry."

"Can nothing be done?"

"I'm afraid not. The snakes are good but they cannot perform miracles."

Gyllbane shut her eyes tight. "Cody and I, we escaped

MacHeath and that was a miracle, and our time together seems like another sort of miracle. But it is over." The sky was growing darker. The stars were breaking out and Gyllbane looked up as if searching for something. Then she rose and walked away. Gylfie fluttered off her back, sensing that the wolf needed to be alone for a while, alone and apart. She went over to where the owls were still clustered around Twilight. The snakes' jaws were stretched so wide open that they appeared to be unhinged. Their forked tongues were flickering in the night like strange pink lightning as they dabbed their venom in the still-bleeding wounds of Twilight. Soren looked up. "I think they're stanching the flow of blood. He seems better. His breathing is more even. But the gash on his port wing is bad. I don't know how he'll fly with it ever again."

A ragged voice cut through the evening air. "I'll teach myself. I'm from the Orphan School of Tough Learning. Flew when I was barely fledged. Nobody taught me then. Had to figure it out for myself. Lived with foxes in Kuneer. Learned how to drill a hole in a tree from woodpeckers in Ambala. I'll teach myself to fly with this wing, you can bet on it. Now, scram, all of you. I need my sleep. I'll be ready to fly by tomorrow's First Black." He paused and churred. "With a little help from my friends."

*   *   *

Twilight was ready not by First Black but two days later, which was miracle enough. The Band arranged themselves into a loose rectangle known as a krokenbot, which was a flight vacuum for transporting wounded owls. It was a formation they had learned from the owls of the Northern Kingdoms and it had proven as effective as the more traditional vine hammocks they often brought to the battlefield. The seven owls, the Band plus Doc Finebeak, Coryn, and Madame Plonk, rose now into the night with Twilight in the middle of the rectangle, who gingerly flapped his wings every few seconds. As they flew, Gylfie spun her head back to look for Gyllbane. The beautiful wolf had climbed to the very top of the rock formation known as the Great Horns, which were two peaks that rose like the tufts of a Great Horned Owl into the sky. The wolf had camped there for a night and a day and now into this night. Like a sentry of the night sky, she kept watch on a track of stars that the wolves called the spirit trail, which led to a constellation known to wolves as the cave of souls. She was waiting for the lochinmorrin, when Cody's spirit would begin to climb the spirit trail to find his peace in the cave of souls. Gyllbane would know it deep within her when it finally happened and she would wait patiently until that moment.

CHAPTER TWENTY-FIVE

Other-ish

"Primrose!" Otulissa said, shocked as the tiny Pygmy Owl was shoved into the prison hollow of the great tree. "What in the world are you doing here?"

"Blasphemy." Primrose sighed.

"Blasphe . . . W-w-w-w-what? What in the world does that mean?" Otulissa asked.

Primrose blinked. "You mean you don't know?" She was stunned. She thought Otulissa, the most learned owl in the tree, would know the meaning of this word. How could Elyan and Gemma know and not Otulissa? They weren't half as smart.

"Well, I am familiar with the word in certain contexts. It comes from the Others and has something to do with their gods and their churches, but it is certainly not an owl word. I can't imagine it being an owl anything."

"Well, it is and I've done it."

"What have you done?"

"Nothing that I am aware of. So I can't really tell you."

"Primrose, Primrose." Otulissa sighed. "Does this have something to do with the ember?"

"Yes, but I didn't cause it."

"I'm sure you didn't. Just begin at the beginning."

"I was on watch. You know I'm" — she paused — "or *was*, an acolyte of the ashes. My duties were to remove the ashes from the chalice."

"The chalice? What in hagsmire is that?"

"You know, the container that Bubo made."

"Since when are they calling it the chalice? We always just called it the container or the pot — or the cask. Another one of those frinkin' Others' words. We're owls, for Glaux's sake, not Others. Well, go on."

"It was shortly after I removed the ashes that the ember started to grow dimmer, lose its glow. To make a long story short, they all got nervous. They were sure that somehow I hadn't done it right, hadn't said the right words."

"What words?"

"Just words. Gemma made them up, I think. She said I'd done something, said them wrong. Saying them wrong is blasphemy. But I swear I said them the way I always did when I remove the ashes. I didn't do anything differently. The ember just started to kind of fade. I didn't make blas-whatever." And with that, the little Pygmy Owl began to weep.

Otulissa hopped over and began running her beak through the feathers on Primrose's tiny wings. "Of course you didn't." She paused and pitched her voice low and very rough. "You want to hear blasphemy? I wish they'd chuck that frinking ember into the Sea of Hoolemere and I'd yarp a pellet on it for good measure!"

Primrose jerked up her head. "Don't speak that way, Otulissa. You'll really get in trouble."

"Trouble? I'm in *prison*. It's the whole frinking tree that's in trouble."

Primrose blinked again. She'd never heard such language coming from Otulissa. She was swearing worse than a seagull.

The prison hollow was not commodious and there had even been talk of putting bars in another hollow as there were apparently more blasphemers. But on this particular morning as a weak winter sun trickled in, Otulissa, who could not sleep, got up to stretch her wings as best she could without disturbing Primrose. Normally, she would have been happy to see this late-winter sun, for that would mean that spring could not be more than a moon cycle away, that the tree would be coming out of the season of the white rain and begin to turn silvery and then with summer golden and then in the final flush of the yearly cycle, copper rose. But for moon cycle after moon cycle, it had not changed. It was still summer gold. *How boring life is when nothing changes,* Otulissa thought as she peered out through the bars. *Gold! I hate it!* Just then in the pale dawn sky that was streaked with a pink as delicate as the inside of seashells, she saw a spot of white — two spots of white. *Not clouds,* she thought. Her thoughts came slowly but with a crispness, a clarity as she watched the two spots grow larger.

It can't be. She hasn't flown out from the island in years. But I swear I'd recognize that fat head anyplace. And Soren! Her gizzard leaped.

In the next moment, a great triumphal chord sounded from the grass harp. The great tree throbbed with a fluttering of wings, and owls could be heard crying, "The Band is back! The king is returning." Hundreds of owls swarmed out of their hollows. The air around the tree was laced with cries of "Hail Coryn, king of the Great Ga'Hoole Tree. The ember will glow once more." Then the sound of things crashing, shattering.

"What was that? What is it?" Primrose awoke with a start.

"Coryn is back. The Band is back," Otulissa said breathlessly.

"But that noise. Is it a fight? What is happening?"

"I don't know." Otulissa blinked. Fear threaded through her gizzard. "I can't imagine."

And Otulissa really couldn't have imagined what was going on in the Great Hollow. The Band, Madame Plonk, Coryn, and Doc Finebeak swept through the immense hollow where the owls shared many of their most solemn and most festive occasions. In their absence, the Great Hollow had been rendered unrecognizable — draped with all sorts of embroidered cloth and tapestries made by the nest-maids' sewing guild. The ember itself had been placed on an altar that was strung with beads and pearls obviously acquired through Trader Mags.

"It looks like a church!" Gylfie squealed in dismay.

"It's so OTHER!" Soren gasped.

"It sure ain't owl!" Twilight raged. Twilight, who had much of his strength back, now seemed suddenly to regain the rest as he flew directly at the tapestry that hung behind the altar and, with his beak, tore it down.

"Blasphemy!" an owl cried. "Arrest that owl!"

"Shut up!" Bubo roared. "Or I'll knock yer block off!"

"Bubo," Coryn commanded, "go immediately and release Otulissa and then take your strongest hammer and tongs and destroy those prison bars."

The Band and Coryn tore through the Great Hollow,

ripping down tapestries, scattering ashes from small cups and bowls. The Guardians of the Guardians of the Ember perched in a confused silence, wilfed, slender shadows of their former selves. They mumbled to one another, blinking and wondering. And when all the gilt and glittering ornamentation had been removed, the Great Hollow stripped bare of its elaborate decoration, the acolytes and the choirs told to shut their beaks and stop the maddening songs and prayers of praise to an ember, Coryn called the owls of the great tree to order.

"The parliament!" the young king commanded. "I want the parliament perched directly before me." The owls of the parliament gathered on a perch. "Now this group, the . . . the . . ." Coryn resisted calling them a mob. "The Guardians of the Guardians of the Ember, please fly forth."

Six owls flew up and lighted down in front of Coryn: Elyan, Gemma, and Yeena; Penfold, a Northern Saw-whet; Humbert, a Spotted Owl; and a Great Gray called Felix.

"Disgrace to the species!" Twilight muttered, eyeing Felix.

Elyan stepped forward. "We meant no harm. We only intended to protect."

"You did nothing of the sort," Coryn fumed. "You violated the very meaning, the essence of this tree. A prison!

What twisted gizzard came up with the horrendous notion of a prison? How dare you!" Coryn flew directly at the six owls, dropped his beak open, and hissed his fury at them. The tiny Northern Saw-whet was toppled by the wash of Coryn's wings flapping in rage. "And this ember!" He seized the iron cask and shook it so the ember glowed more fiercely. "This ember is not a living thing. It has heat, yes, and peculiar powers, and must be kept from the likes of Nyra. But it is not noble. You Guardians are noble. And I set the Great Ga'Hoole Tree and its noble owls above any ember. It is your loyalty, your love of this tree and its values that I esteem above any riches in the owl kingdoms. For that is invaluable and knows no price. I shall take the ember back to the Beyond if it becomes a false god to you. We are owls. We value each other. We celebrate our owlness and not the heat and the glow of an ember. You have done shameful things, committed heinous acts in the name of this ember. You have imprisoned one of our most trusted and revered owls, the ryb Otulissa. You have forced Bubo to make bars for a prison. Arrest!" Coryn spat out the word. "We have no room for such words in our good and Great Tree of Ga'Hoole."

"What will you do to us?" Felix asked. "What is our punishment?" Coryn blinked at the six owls. They all were waiting for him to mete out some punishment. But that would be too easy. "What would you want me to do? Put you in prison?" he said with a contempt that made every owl's gizzard shrink in shame. "What has happened here?" he wondered aloud. "You have become so Other-ish. Perhaps you should go to a place where Others might live. But they live no longer, as I understand. Now go to your hollows. We will deal with you later."

The offending owls filed out.

Coryn picked up the teacup and looked at the picture of the dignified queen with her serene blue eyes. Queen E. "Here, Madame Plonk, this belongs to you, I believe."

"I don't want it any longer, Your Majesty."

"No, Plonkie," Coryn called to her affectionately. "Take it. It is yours. You have never confused being an owl with being an Other. You're owl, through and through."

"Take it, my dear," Doc Finebeak urged.

Coryn motioned the Band and Otulissa to follow him to his hollow.

Otulissa's eyes immediately fell on the tattered book. She walked up to it slowly as she might cautiously approach a poisonous snake she was not quite sure was dead.

"It's not *The Book of Kreeth*? Great Glaux!" she whispered.

"It is," Soren replied quietly. "Nyra had it."

Otulissa jerked her head up in horror and blinked rapidly. "Let's hope she didn't learn too much."

"We want you to take a look at it," Coryn said. "You, of all of us, understand Krakish best."

Hesitantly, she opened the book as if she expected venom to shoot from it. The minutes slipped by silently, slowly. The owls almost dared not breathe. Finally, Otulissa looked up. "Well, the good news is that Nyra could not have understood a word of this. The bad news is that I can't, either. It is very ancient Krakish. We don't even have the dictionaries here that might help me with translation."

"Where would you find them?" Twilight asked.

Otulissa looked at Coryn and then Soren. "Does Coryn know about Bess?" she whispered.

"The Knower?" Coryn asked excitedly. "The Boreal Owl in the Palace of Mists?"

"I guess you do," Otulissa said matter-of-factly. "She is the only one who could decipher this. Some of it, I daresay, is written in code. But Bess is experienced with codes."

"You mean we have to go to the Palace of Mists?" Gylfie said.

"In time, I imagine," Otulissa replied. "But for now let's keep the book a secret."

"Ezylryb's secret library," Soren suggested.

"Maybe," Otulissa said. "But first I think we need to hide the ember." Its reddish light danced on the walls. The glow had been restored to an even greater intensity. Red shadows sprang across the walls as if in a wanton and wild dance to unheard music.

"And you have some ideas about that?" Coryn asked.

"Yes, come closer, all of you — not a word beyond this hollow."

Then in the ear slits of the Band, Otulissa whispered her plan.

Epilogue

On another part of the Island of Hoole, not far from the great tree, as the sun rode high in the lengthening days of early spring and the inhabitants of the tree slept the thick sleep of midday, Coryn, the Band, and Otulissa gathered deep in the cave of Bubo the blacksmith.

"This here be where I keep them." Bubo the Great Horned nodded at pits in the cave floor that glowed with heaps of coals. "I got me bonks right here." He pointed with a sooty talon. "And then the others — grade A, grade B, I don't go lower than C. Below C, they ain't much good for anything."

He paused and chuckled. "'Course, with colliers like Soren and Otulissa, Ruby and Martin, it be mostly bonks and grade A I get." This was not flattery but the truth. The colliering chaw was extraordinarily talented. Not only were they good at retrieving coals, they were excellent teachers. Soren's mate, Pelli, was bringing in a fair share of bonk coals recently, as was a young Saw-whet that Martin was teaching to work the lower layers of forest fires. "So, you be thinking of keeping the Ember of Hoole in here?"

"It was Otulissa's idea and I think it is a good one," Soren said.

"The idea is that the ember should never again become an object of . . . of . . . of fascination, of worship." Gylfie's voice was urgent as she spoke these words.

"We know it is not like other coals or embers," Coryn continued. "It affects owls who come into its presence differently." *And sometimes even those who are not in its presence,* he thought. He would never forget the extraordinary heat that began to burn within him as Nyra advanced against him, pressing him into that sheer rock wall in the canyonlands. He remembered the shock when he realized that the green light that he was seeing was actually coming from his own eyes. No one else had witnessed this, no one except Nyra, and she had appeared to have gone yeep and then simply vanished.

By careful questioning of Primrose, Coryn had figured out that it was exactly at the moment of this confrontation with Nyra that the ember's glow had begun to fade and this was what had led to Primrose's arrest. Through some mystical transference, the ember's energy had briefly become his. And although he had survived, as far as he knew his mother was not dead. Merely vanished. No body, no bones, no remains to be burned. He had peered into a few fires since he had returned, attempting to scour the flames for clues to what had happened to her. It was foolish, of course, because Coryn knew that he could never go to a fire and demand such specific information. He coughed a bit now as if to clear his head of the thought. "But Bubo, you do not seem to be affected by the ember."

"I been around so many most all me life, maybe it's . . . it's . . ."

"Like an immunity," Otulissa added. "You know, if you have had mite blight three or four times, your feathers somehow grow used to it and pretty soon the mites just dry up and don't hurt your feathers at all."

"Maybe that's it," Bubo said. "But you're welcome to keep the ember here. I can't think of a better place to hide it than in plain sight with a mess of other coals. No special container."

"Well, it was a brilliant idea, thanks to Otulissa." Soren nodded at the Spotted Owl. "Coryn, why don't you remove it now and put it in with the rest of Bubo's bonk coals?"

"Happily," Coryn said.

He plucked open the latch of the teardrop-shaped container with his talons. The ember had regained its glow since their return. It looked as it always had, fiercely orange with the glimmer of green surrounding the lick of blue at its center. Except for the green it was not so different from any of the other bonk coals in the pit. And that was exactly how the owls in Bubo's cave wanted it. There would be no more special groups or orders or societies or Guardians of the Guardians of the Ember. Coryn tipped the container over the pit and the Ember of Hoole tumbled in, lodging amid a cluster of embers in the top layer. Then it dropped down until it was almost out of sight among the others. All of the owls felt a gentle stirring like the softest breeze passing through their gizzards. They looked slowly at one another and knew at last that their world had been restored, their great tree put to rights — owls among owls and an ember among embers.

That evening as the owls began to rouse themselves from their sleep, across the Sea of Hoolemere, in the canyonlands, a beautiful wolf cast her wild untamed song into a night that flowed with stars as she saw a gathering of soft mist, the creamy golden color of her own coat.

"Cody!" she whispered. The mist wolf turned his head and raised its muzzle as if to say good-bye. "Go on! Go on!" she urged, and she felt something in her let go. Gyllbane could rest now; her pup was on the star trail and had nearly reached the cave of souls.

OWLS
and others from the

GUARDIANS OF GA'HOOLE SERIES

The Band

SOREN: Barn Owl, *Tyto alba*, from the Forest Kingdom of Tyto; escaped from St. Aegolius Academy for Orphaned Owls; a Guardian at the Great Ga'Hoole Tree and close advisor to the king

GYLFIE: Elf Owl, *Micrathene whitneyi*, from the Desert Kingdom of Kuneer; escaped from St. Aegolius Academy for Orphaned Owls; Soren's best friend; a Guardian at the Great Ga'Hoole Tree and ryb of navigation chaw

TWILIGHT: Great Gray Owl, *Strix nebulosa*, free flier, orphaned within hours of hatching; Guardian at the Great Ga'Hoole Tree

DIGGER: Burrowing Owl, *Athene cunicularia*, from the Desert Kingdom of Kuneer; lost in the desert after attack in which his brother was killed by owls from St. Aegolius; a Guardian at the Great Ga'Hoole Tree

The Leaders of the Great Ga'Hoole Tree

CORYN: Barn Owl, *Tyto alba*, the new young king of the great tree; son of Nyra, leader of the Pure Ones

EZYLRYB: Whiskered Screech Owl, *Otus trichopsis*, Soren's former mentor; the wise, much-loved, departed ryb at the Great Ga'Hoole Tree (also known as LYZE OF KIEL)

Others at the Great Ga'Hoole Tree

OTULISSA: Spotted Owl, *Strix occidentalis*, chief ryb, and ryb of Ga'Hoology and weather chaws; an owl of great learning and prestigious lineage

MARTIN: Northern Saw-whet Owl, *Aegolius acadicus*, member of the Chaw of Chaws; a Guardian at the Great Ga'Hoole Tree

RUBY: Short-eared Owl, *Asio flammeus*, member of the Chaw of Chaws; a Guardian at the Great Ga'Hoole Tree

EGLANTINE: Barn Owl, *Tyto alba*, Soren's younger sister

MADAME PLONK: Snowy Owl, *Nyctea scandiaca*, the elegant singer of the Great Ga'Hoole Tree

MRS. PLITHIVER: blind snake, formerly the nest-maid for Soren's family; now a member of the harp guild at the Great Ga'Hoole Tree

OCTAVIA: Kielian snake, nest-maid for many years for Madame Plonk and Ezylryb (also known as BRIGID)

GEMMA: Whiskered Screech Owl, *Otus trichopsis,* a pompous member of the Great Ga'Hoole Tree

ELYAN: Great Gray Owl, *Strix nebulosa,* a member of the parliament who is unwholesomely in thrall to the Ember of Hoole

Characters from the Time of the Legends

GRANK: Spotted Owl, *Strix occidentalis,* the first collier; friend to young King H'rath and Queen Siv during their youth; first owl to find the ember

HOOLE: Spotted Owl, *Strix occidentalis,* son of H'rath; retriever of the Ember of Hoole; founder and first king of the great tree

H'RATH: Spotted Owl, *Strix occidentalis,* King of the N'yrthghar, a frigid region known in later times as the Northern Kingdoms; father of Hoole

SIV: Spotted Owl, *Strix occidentalis,* mate of H'rath and Queen of the N'yrthghar, a frigid region known in later times as the Northern Kingdoms; mother of Hoole

KREETH: Female hagsfiend with strong powers of nachtmagen; friend of Ygryk; conjured Lutta into being

Other Characters

DUNLEAVY MacHEATH: treacherous dire wolf, once leader of the MacHeath clan in Beyond the Beyond

GYLLBANE: courageous member of the MacHeath clan of dire wolves; her pup, Cody, was maimed by clan leader Dunleavy MacHeath

BESS: Boreal Owl, *Aegolius funerus*, daughter of Grimble, who was a guard at St. Aegolius Academy for Orphaned Owls; keeper of the Palace of Mists (also known as THE KNOWER)

DOC FINEBEAK: Snowy Owl, *Nyctea scandiaca*, famed freelance tracker once in the employ of the Pure Ones

Coming soon!

GUARDIANS OF GA'HOOLE

BOOK THIRTEEN

The River of Wind

by Kathryn Lasky

Coryn and the Band have returned to the Great Ga'Hoole Tree and restored order. With the ember safely hidden away, the tree shakes off its gaudy golden glow and recovers its natural majesty. Meanwhile, deep in the Palace of Mists, Bess finds an ancient map fragment that reveals that there are not five owl kingdoms as has been thought since time immemorial — but six. Coryn and the Chaw of Chaws set off to find this unknown realm. In a landscape of endless wonders they discover a monastery of mysterious, learned blue-eyed owls, the like of which no one has ever before seen.

While they explore the unknown, the young Guardians Primrose and Eglantine fly on a rescue mission to the known kingdoms. Far from home they uncover a plot by Nyra and the remnant Pure Ones to assassinate the young king and his noble companions. It is too late to get help from the Guardians back at the tree. Primrose and Eglantine must race against time itself to find the strange unknown land and warn Coryn before the Pure Ones find — and kill — them.